The Chocolate Cure

The Chocolate Cure

A Love at the Chocolate Shop Romance

Roxanne Snopek

Oct1/1? Golden Ears Festival
For Gerry!
Enjoy the
chocolate!
:)

Roxanne Snopek

TULE
PUBLISHING

Dedication

To Ray, as always.

Acknowledgments

With thanks to Sinclair Sawhney and her brilliant editorial eye, the entire Tule Team for their support and especially my Chocolate Shop collaborators: CJ Carmichael, who invited me into this fantastic project, Melissa McClone, Debra Salonen, Marin Thomas and Steena Holmes. It's been great working with you all! Chocolate, forever!

In addition to the above, I'm grateful to several other eagle-eyed and enthusiastic readers: Stephanie Snopek, Andrea Snopek, Connie Jones, Paula Altenburg and Laura Kyte. You each brought a unique perspective to the story that greatly strengthened the end result – THANK YOU!!! Any mistakes remaining are mine alone.

No more chocolate! No more meddling! No more men!

New Year's resolutions are great. Announcing them in a crowded bar, with a chocolate martini in her hand? Not Maddie Cash's finest moment. It's time this new realtor got serious about her life and this time, she means it.

But when hospital volunteering lands her at the bedside of bruised and battered Mick Meyer, who has no knowledge of Maddie's reputation – and no memory of the kiss he begged from her during that long, pain-filled night, her best-laid plans are put in jeopardy. It's not just his sweet tooth that's tempting her.

The hunky bush pilot with the concussion has an old family property to unload. Making this sale could be Maddie's professional salvation. But when Mick turns on the charm, she's in danger of forgetting all her best intentions... on chocolate... on meddling... and especially on men.

Chapter One

"THE USUAL, MADDIE?" the bartender asked.

Madeleine Cash tossed her hair away from her face where it was endangering her false eyelashes, and blotted her damp forehead with the back of her hand. The cold from the snow swirling and drifting outside did nothing to cut the warmth of the busy saloon.

"Not yet, Jason. Sparkling water with a slice of lime, please." If there was ever an occasion for her to enjoy a chocolate martini, it was New Year's Eve, at Grey's Saloon, surrounded by friends and family. But she was the first of them to arrive, which was a bummer, and she wasn't yet in a celebratory mood.

In fact, she was in a bit of a funk.

Maddie wasn't accustomed to worrying. The mere fact of this funk... was worrying in itself.

Plus, she always got a little... glowy... when she indulged in alcohol. Funky plus glowy could only equal trouble.

"Give her a chocolate martini," a voice at her elbow said.

"My treat."

"Forget it, Tod." She leaned sideways, nudging her coworker with her shoulder to soften her words. "I'm being a good girl tonight."

"I'm counting on it."

"Ick. I'm telling Elinor. She'll take away your allowance."

With his expensive haircuts and perfect clothes, Tod Styles was handsome enough. But even she knew better than to dabble with her boss's son, especially now.

Elinor was implementing cost cutting measures and, as she'd kindly but clearly pointed out, Maddie's dramatic tearing up of Rosie Linn's contract had put a significant dent in the last quarter sales figures. It wasn't her place to make magnanimous gestures, no matter how well-intentioned.

Plus, Tod's lips reminded her of watermelon gummy worms.

"Half the men here are counting on it." Jason Grey pushed a paper coaster in front of her and set her drink on it.

"And look at how responsible I'm being." She lifted the glass at Jason and Tod in turn, then took a delicate sip. "A mature, professional woman, here to ring in the new year with friends. In a mature, professional way. No flirting with the help."

"You could no more give up vodka and flirting than you could give up chocolate," Jason said.

"Why would I want to give up any of that? I embrace life. Chocolate and men are part of that."

"And vodka," Tod said.

"Nope." At least, not until her friends arrived.

"I'm not saying you should give up anything," Jason said. "I'm saying you couldn't if you tried."

"I could so!"

Okay, she had a tab at Grey's. Who didn't? And of course Copper Mountain Chocolates had her credit card on file. Sage's chocolate was the best in the state. The world. The universe.

As for men, well. She was alive, wasn't she?

Jason moved away to fill another order and Tod turned to flirt with the girl on his other side.

Annoyed, Maddie took another sip, her lips leaving a pretty smudge of Candy Coral Kiss on the glass. Fizzy bubbles sparkled their zero-calorie dance on her tongue. This wasn't so bad. Who were they to imply she had no self-control?

She knew how to enjoy life. That was a good thing.

Moderation, however, wasn't her strong suit.

A sweet-smelling arm draped lightly over her shoulder, turning into a tight side-hug.

"Cynthia!" Maddie shifted to make room. "You're here! I'm so glad. We're going to have so much fun tonight."

Since the day they'd met, Maddie had adored her stepsister, she of the braces and the stutter and the low self-esteem just waiting for the encouragement of an older sister or two. Cynthia was preparing for a spring wedding with her fiancé,

Chad, and happiness shone from every last bit of her.

Cynthia deserved it and Maddie was one hundred percent thrilled for her.

"You look so nice," Cynthia said.

"Thanks." Maddie glanced down at her simple black dress. Too simple, at least for her. But her boss had also suggested a more professional appearance.

That had stung. Elinor was so lovely and polished, her gentle critique of Maddie's flair came as a shock.

For someone whose last name was Styles, she was disappointingly narrow-minded in her appreciation of what that entailed.

"Are you meeting someone?" Cynthia asked.

"Nope. It's just me."

"And me." Tod leered hopefully at Maddie.

"Not at gunpoint, Toddler."

He glowered.

Maddie leaned over the bar. Where was Jason? "You're all sex-goddess gorgeous, yourself. Watch out, Tod's going to fall into your cleavage and then Chad's going to go all caveman on him."

"I can take Chad," Tod said.

Cynthia caught Jason's eye, pointed to Maddie's drink and held up two fingers. "No worries, Chad's not coming tonight. He and the guys are away at his stag."

"Right, I forgot."

Chad was celebrating with a bunch of pals from Marietta, all of whom shared a love for restoring old houses. And all of whom were ridiculously fine-looking men. Watching them work gave new meaning to the term house porn. Especially when they took their shirts off.

Too bad they were all married, more or less.

"Four days at some rundown camp. Super rustic, which is like catnip to them." Cynthia shuddered. "One of Chad's friends just inherited it and wanted them to check it out with him. Mick Meyer. I met him. He's hot."

"Cowboy hot? Or hot-hot? Not that there's anything wrong with cowboys," Maddie added quickly. Chad was a cowboy. As was his brother Eric. As were ninety percent of the men in Marietta. Eighty percent of whom she'd dated already.

A nice clean-cut, Armani-wearing, hedge-fund manager, that was what she wanted. Ha.

"Bush pilot hot," Cynthia said. "They're ice-fishing. Can you imagine?"

"In this weather? Better them than me." A thought occurred to her. "That means it's just us girls. On New Year's Eve. Best night ever!"

"Sorry, sis. Apparently, you have to take out a second mortgage to get a sitter on December 31."

"Not even Samara?"

Melinda and Leda each had preschoolers but Samara's daughter, Jade, was at least six now. Surely Sam had found someone to stay with her.

But Cynthia shook her head.

"Spawn." Maddie huffed. "They ruin everything."

It sucked being single when everyone around her was oozing domestic bliss and popping out adorable little spit factories every time she turned around.

Jason pushed two sweating glasses of sparkling water with lime toward them.

"Actually, we'll have a couple of white wine spritzers," Maddie called. But the bartender was already gone.

"It's okay," said Cynthia. "This is perfect."

"No way. We deserve a little something, being abandoned as we are."

Cynthia bit her lip and glanced away. Then met Maddie's eyes and took a deliberate sip of her fizzy water.

Maddie looked at the drink, then up at Cynthia's face. Maddie's jaw dropped.

"Cynthia! Are you—" She clapped a hand over her mouth.

She didn't want to jinx anything. She also needed to keep her heart from leaping straight out of her chest to flop onto the bar top.

A Cynthia-Chad baby would be the most adorable, sweetest, heaven-sent treasure in the entire world.

"Don't say it." Cynthia glared at her and then glanced meaningfully at the people surrounding them. "It's too early to talk about it. So, no."

"But maybe?" she whispered.

Cynthia bit her lip. Then she smiled. "Maybe."

Maddie shrieked and hollered. "Happy New Year! I'm going to be—"

"Kicked out," Jason said. "Cynthia, keep her in line, will you?"

"No problem." Cynthia dragged her off her seat by the arm and led her to a quieter corner. "You're impossible."

"Need some help?" Tod said, reappearing at her elbow with a glass of wine in each hand.

Maddie grabbed one. "Family stuff, Tod. Private family stuff."

Cynthia thanked Tod but declined the glass.

"Does DeeDee know?" Maddie whispered.

Deirdre, Maddie's twin sister, was a model in New York City and had been steadily and determinedly drifting away from the family, another thing on Maddie's list of things not to worry about tonight.

"No. Nor do Dad and Joanie. And don't you tell them. I'll make an announcement when the time is right." Cynthia twinkled. "Got that, Aunt Maddie?"

Aunt Maddie.

She liked the sound of that. A big, rollicking family full of laughter and love, all of them getting together at the farm, Mom and Norm putting all the leaves in the table to accommodate everyone at mealtime.

Assuming Norm would still be around to see it.

Don't think about that tonight. Don't think about anything tonight.

Darn, that list was tough to ignore.

Maddie gulped down her drink, tossed her hair over her shoulder and pulled Cynthia out of the corner. "Why isn't anyone dancing? We'll be the first. Someone's got to get this party started."

Jason turned up the music and Maddie gave herself over to the pure joy of sound and movement and the crush of people. So not everyone was here tonight. She had plenty of friends. She had a family she loved, and would soon see an addition. She had a good job, at the moment. And if that disappeared, she'd find another.

She tipped her head back and whirled in a circle, her hips moving in time to the beat of Keith Urban's "The Fighter". She had so much to be grateful for. Marietta was the best place in the world and she had such a great life.

"I'd be your fighter, Cynthia," she yelled.

"I'm Tod," Tod said into her ear. "You can fight for me."

"Nope," she said. "Inappropriate fraternization."

She had a job she enjoyed. She'd fight for that, if she had to.

Elinor wouldn't really fire her.

"If you can say words like that, you need this." Tod pressed a chocolate-drizzled martini glass into her hand.

She sniffed it. Cocoa and vanilla. Divine. Maybe she did need it. Where was Cynthia, anyway? The bathroom, probably. Or maybe she left when Maddie started dancing.

She took the glass. Downed it.

"Don't get any ideas," she said, shoving the empty glass at him. "I don't need a man to have fun, especially not you."

There was nothing wrong with being single.

Nothing.

"Hear me roar!" she yelled.

Laughter surrounded her, enveloped her, embraced her. Cynthia might have ditched Maddie, but that didn't mean she was alone.

In fact, as the clock wound down to midnight, she found herself talking and dancing with so many generous and appreciative men who kept things interesting, and made sure to keep her drinks refreshed, that she couldn't remember why she'd ever imagined herself to be lonely.

"Ten... nine... eight..."

She wasn't lonely.

"Seven... six... five..."

She threw her arms around the nearest available man. She was celebrating New Year's Eve and the fresh start of a new and better year.

A new and better life.

A new and better *her.*

"GOOD MORNING, HAPPY New Year, wakey-wakey, time to get up, brunch awaits!" said Joanie Cash-Henley. "And this little sweetheart is about out of patience."

The edge of the mattress dipped as Maddie's relentlessly cheerful mother leaned over to pull the blankets away from Maddie's face and plunked four pounds of hair and attitude onto the sheet beside her.

Clementine.

A snuffling, cold, wet nose pressed against her cheek, followed by the scrabble of tiny claws as the lonely little Yorkshire terrier mix she'd adopted in November burrowed beneath the covers.

"We adore dog-sitting, as you know, but she's a handful and I think she wore Norman out last night."

Home, home on the ranch. Where the guilt and the martyrdom play.

"Five more minutes. I beg you."

"It's the first day of the rest of your life, darling," Joanie said. "Turkey bacon and grilled tomatoes is just the ticket."

Her gut lurched. "Trust me, it's not."

The aroma of coffee wafted through the muddy swamp of alcohol, trans fats, and regret in which simmered what was left of her brain.

And hit her stomach.

"Mom." She groaned into her pillow. "Let me die in peace."

Question—why, why, why hadn't she gone back to her own place for the night? *Home sweet apartment. Where you're free to stay in bed all day, if you wanted.*

Which she did.

Bigger question—why, why, why had she gone to Grey's Saloon for New Year's Eve? She should have gone to the Masked Ball and been classy. Then she remembered that she'd had neither ticket nor date. Okay, well, she could have been responsible and curled up with Mom and Norm and Clem to watch the ball drop. A little Scrabble, a little ginger ale, a few toasts to the upcoming demise of what she'd thought might actually be a career.

Who was she kidding? The hangover had been inevitable.

Maddie heard a ruffling, snapping sound. Sunlight flooded the room, stabbing her skull, despite the pillow. She pulled her knees up and curled into herself. This was Dee-Dee's fault. If she'd come home for the holidays, like a good daughter, their mother's ferocious care and attention would have had its laser-like intensity split between two targets.

"It's nearly noon," Joanie said. "Your dad needs to eat."

"Then feed him. He doesn't need me."

"Of course he does. We cherish having you here, dear. We want to enjoy every minute. I've made that streusel-topped coffee cake you love."

Manipulation, laced with brown sugar and cinnamon. Joanie was in top form.

She heard Joanie's footsteps move toward the door, finally. "I'll bring you some coffee. That'll help."

"I doubt it." Maddie yanked the covers back over her head in a vain attempt to block out the tractor-beam of winter-white Montana sunshine, as relentless as her mother.

Clementine licked Maddie's chin. Then nibbled.

Darn it. There was no denying the return of consciousness. Maddie flung the covers back, dragged her purse off the night table, and fumbled around inside for the package of dark chocolate covered salted caramels she kept there. In case of emergency.

Three left. Thank the sweet baby Jesus.

Baby.

Wait.

Maddie squinted at Clementine, willing her to speak. Clementine blinked brightly back at her.

Cynthia.

Cynthia was pregnant!

In love, getting married, pregnant.

Maddie's eyes burned. She was so, so happy for Cynthia. One hundred percent happy.

Well, ninety percent happy, ten percent envious.

For a moment, she stared at the chocolate, pondering the idea of restraint, which she thought showed great strength of character in and of itself.

But the pink salt crystals glinted at her so invitingly and, heck, if getting reprimanded on the last day of work before the holidays wasn't reason to indulge, what was?

Eight months with Styles Realty, the longest she'd ever held a job in her life. She really, really didn't want to lose it.

She took a nibble, imagining a smooth, dark trail coating

her insides, soothing, protecting.

Who needed milk of magnesia? Chocolate was her cure. For everything.

Not today, apparently.

Maddie flopped backwards and pulled the edges of her pillow over her face. Her head hurt, her stomach churned, her legs ached, her heart burned.

It was like a bad country song.

After Cynthia left, Maddie's memories of the New Year's Eve party got blurry. There'd been wine, no doubt about that. Vanilla vodka, too. Dancing, definitely. Music, of course. A crowded dance floor. Men, as usual. She groaned. Self-control? She'd drunk too much, eaten too much, flirted too much.

She crammed the rest of the chocolate into her mouth.

Come on, endorphins!

She flopped onto her other side. She'd made a fool of herself last night, almost certainly.

Ten... nine... eight... seven...

Maddie hadn't been alone at the stroke of midnight.

Go back to sleep. Don't think about it and it'll all go away.

But the memories became clearer now, the sugar rush lifting her brain fog.

A sloppy kiss, sweaty hands on the back of her neck, the stale odor of beer and lime and greasy chicken wings and... gummy worms?

She'd been having fun, enjoying the party, exactly as she

was supposed to be doing. She was very deliberately not thinking about DeeDee, so far away, or envying Cynthia, or worrying about Norm's heart or bemoaning the fact that she, a mid-twenties woman – okay, edging to late-twenties but who was counting? – didn't have anyone special to kiss under the mistletoe and might not even have a job, soon.

No, Maddie had not been thinking about all those things, because she'd been busy getting tipsy. It was New Year's Eve, after all. It was allowed.

And at the stroke of midnight, she'd found someone to kiss because that was allowed, too. It was almost a rule.

The door to her room opened with a crash. Clementine leaped to her feet, her yapping like a stiletto against Maddie's brittle brain.

"Get up, Madeleine," said Joanie. "No more wallowing. Oh, Lordy. You didn't wash your face before you went to bed, did you?"

"Raccoon eyes?"

"All over the pillow. You should see your hair, too. What a picture. A long, hot shower is what you need."

Maddie's ever-loving mother hauled the blankets off the bed entirely, Clementine with them.

"It's bad enough that the whole town saw you with your tongue down your boss's son's throat last night."

Oh. God. Tod.

It was worse than she'd thought.

"But no," Joanie continued, "you had to get up on the

bar and announce to everyone and their chickens exactly how you intend to become the new, improved Maddie Cash."

Oh.

"And, oh, my goodness." Joanie's voice rose in that special mix of parental disapproval and incredulity that made Maddie want to stab herself in the eardrum. "Madeleine Elizabeth Cash, is that... chocolate?"

She grabbed the little cellophane package lying next to her purse on the night table and shook the last precious piece into her open palm.

"Actually," said Maddie, "it's a Himalayan salted caramel."

"Less than twelve hours," said Joanie, obviously uninterested in Maddie's prevarications, "and you've already broken your first resolution?"

Maddie almost laughed. Resolutions? She didn't make resolutions.

Wait.

"That's right," said Joanie. "Not only did you make a spectacle of yourself last night – as I've been informed by Carol Bingley already this morning and who knows where she heard it from – but you vowed, in front of God and half of Marietta, to give up chocolate."

Maddie groaned again as the memory snapped into focus, sharp as the icicles glistening outside her window.

"That's right. Chocolate. And meddling. And men.

Which made Tod howl, let me tell you." Joanie folded her arms and shook her head. Then she seemed to wilt, and that tiny gesture made Maddie want to cry. She'd embarrassed her mother. Again.

She was a disappointment. A joke. To her family and herself.

"Oh, Mom," she whispered. Clem whined.

Instantly, Joanie was at her side. Maddie curled into the familiar embrace, knowing she was way too old for it, but needing it nonetheless.

"My girl." Joanie rocked her from side to side. "Whatever am I going to do with you?"

And right then and there, Maddie decided it was time to grow up.

Finally.

Chapter Two

TWO DAYS LATER, at the Marietta hospital emergency room, at the exact moment the swinging doors opened wide, a stainless steel bedpan whipped through them, past Maddie, and crashed into the wall, barely missing her head.

It was a scene straight out of a *Grey's Anatomy* season-ender. Bright lights, noise, pastel and white-coated people rushing about. Street-clothed people standing, sitting, or lying. The automatic doors at the back letting in gusts of frigid air along with uniformed paramedics with clipboards and urgent expressions.

Medical drama looked like a lot more fun on TV than in real life.

The doors closed. Maddie straightened up and lowered her arms, her pulse thumping, endlessly grateful that the bedpan had been empty. Perhaps hospital volunteering had not been the ideal path to follow in her quest for self-improvement. It was fine when she was fluffing pillows and filling vases on the medical ward, or showing them pictures of Clementine.

But she hadn't counted on getting sent to the emergency room.

Sober second thought sucked. She turned back to the waiting room.

Sober first thought. That was what she needed.

"Maddie? What are you doing here? Are you okay?"

She glanced down the hallway to see her future brother-in-law approaching, concern etched on his handsome face. Behind him, in the waiting room, stood the rest of the guys, all scruffy-jawed, hunched in plaid shirts and down jackets, their heavy winter boots leaving droplets of snow melt on the polished floor.

Oh no!

Chad's stag party. She rushed to him. "What happened? Are you okay?"

"I'm fine." Chad gave her a quick hug. "It's our pilot buddy. You know how flight attendants tell you to stay buckled in until the aircraft has come to a complete halt? This is why. He was going to fly out in the morning, but wanted to move his plane to better shelter for the night, because of the storm. He was taxiing – not even flying – when a gust caught his wing. Plane slid around like an egg in butter, hit some rocks or something and he got bounced out onto the ice. Doesn't sound like much but it was pretty impressive at the time."

"Oh, my God! Cynthia told me about him. Mick, right? Is he going to be okay?"

"Banged his head and shoulder pretty badly, but other than that, we think so. We're waiting for an update."

"What an awful end to your stag."

"He's tough. And now we've got a great story."

"I hope he sees it that way. Wow. You're ripe, my friend." She wrinkled her nose. Chad stank of wood smoke, wet dog, and guys-weekend hygiene.

"Mick's uncle's lodge is very basic."

"No plumbing, I take it."

"It's not a proper fishing trip otherwise." Chad eyed her with a frown. "Are you sure you're okay? You don't look well."

"Gee, thanks."

She'd pinned her hair up in a tidy bun at the crown of her head and the only makeup she was wearing was a light skim of tinted moisturizer. She'd even bought a pair of hideous, multi-colored Dansko nursing clogs. Dress the part, be the part, as DeeDee would say.

"I'm volunteering."

He laughed, then saw her face. "Oh. You're serious. Good for you, Maddie. I'm impressed. Hey, maybe you can find out how he's doing? We've been here for over an hour."

The swinging doors crashed open again. Maddie leaped over to hold the doors open as a young woman backed through, pulling a wheeled bed containing an elderly man toward the elevator.

"Little help here!" a voice from the triage bay yelled.

"Hey, Vogue, quit admiring your manicure and give us a hand."

Chad gave her a nudge. "He's talking to you. Go on. I'll see you later."

"I don't know…"

Chad went back to his friends. Maddie stood in the doorway, clenching and unclenching her fists, wondering how the guy in the scrub top had seen her gel tips from all the way over there.

"Anytime now would be great, blondie," Scrub-Top said. "Whoa, buddy, lie still. We need to look at that head lac."

Uh-oh. She recognized the nurse from when she broke her ankle a couple of years ago. Dave. He clearly didn't remember her, which was just as well, as her foggy recollections were mostly of how very, very kissy the drugs had made her feel.

"Whenever you're ready, sweetheart," Dave yelled again, grabbing at his patient. "Buddy, you're asking to be tied down."

Nurse Dave certainly inspired no kissy-feelings now.

"I'm coming," she said.

She was here to help, so she'd help. She picked up the bed pan with two fingers and carried it gingerly to the nursing station.

Dave was leaning over a man on a stretcher, holding him down, while pointing to an old woman in a wheelchair and calling out to other pastel-garbed hospital staff members.

Scraps of conversation wafted her way.

Multi-vehicle accident on I-90, ETA twenty...

Eighty-two-year old female, found wandering outside her home, hypothermic, disoriented times three...

Single occupant ground-level airplane accident... patient unconscious at the scene, now altered, combative... shoulder deformity, possible orbital fracture...

Dr. Jack Gallagher jogged past her, heading for the chaotic scene. Jack had treated Maddie's stepfather during his recent heart attack and she and her family had become fond of him.

"Hey, Maddie. You look different." He frowned at the tag pinned to her blue smock. "You're not volunteering here. Are you?"

Jack didn't need to sound quite so incredulous.

"I am." She smoothed her hands over the shapeless outfit identifying her as a helpful, kind-hearted person.

"Not so's you'd notice," Dave snapped, shoving an IV pole out of his patient's reach. "Watch it, Doc, he's only got one good arm, but it's a doozy."

The patient was big, rugged, with a scruff of beard on his rough-hewn jaw, dark hair sticking up around the pillow. If this was Mick, she could honestly report to Chad that he was alive and kicking.

"I can see this is a bad time," Maddie said. Bad time, bad idea. Bad shoe investment.

"Hold this." Dave shoved the metal pole at her. "Stand here."

So much for a quick getaway. She took a half-step closer to the man who lay writhing on the bed.

His green checked flannel shirt was open to the waistband of his jeans, revealing a lean, well-muscled chest and visible abs. Sun browned skin, strong bones... and blood.

Lots of blood.

Maddie's stomach turned over. A deep gash split one of his eyebrows and the whole side of his face was puffy. Blood covered his pillow and smeared the sheets and clothing and the sweet, metallic odor combined with the funk of an outdoorsman in need of a shower, made her regret her last meal. And that shoulder looked very... wrong.

"Is this Mick?"

The man's eyes sprang open, piercing hers with a mute plea. For a desperate moment, the intensity of his pain and fear flooded over her and, in its wake, helplessness. There was nothing she could do, but oh, how she wished there was.

Then his head lolled backward and his eyes closed.

"You know each other?" Dave said, surprised.

Maddie swallowed, willing herself to be calm. "No. He's my stepsister Cynthia's fiancé's friend. He was here for Chad's stag. Chad and the guys are in the waiting room, wondering how he's doing. Can I take them a message?"

That would be helpful. Cowardly. But still helpful.

"Later. Keep that line out of the way or it'll get caught. Here."

Dave slapped a sealed package of clear plastic tubing into

her hand.

This definitely wasn't what she signed on for. "Maybe I should find someone else. I'm not really qualified."

Those ugly Dansko clogs should have been her first clue. This was so not her.

"On a night like this??" Dave said. "Short-staffed? You won't even get time to pee. Hang onto the pole. And get me the restraints."

The patient they were holding down – Mick – took a shuddering breath. "You smell good," he muttered, "like chocolate."

Maddie touched her pocket. She'd brought a small bag of chocolate-covered caramels with her. Not to eat. Just for… comfort.

"Do you know your name, sir?" Jack lifted the man's lids and peered in with a small flashlight.

The patient wrenched his head away from the light, swearing.

"Concussion," Jack said. "Let's raise him forty-five, on my count. One, two."

They lifted the head of the gurney. Mick howled and flailed one arm wildly, knocking against the IV pole and making the gurney rock.

"Restraints! Now!" Dave jabbed his index finger at a counter, where numerous foreign items lay jumbled together. "Those ties, right there, in front of you."

She grabbed a pile of flesh-colored fabric belts. "These?"

Jack and Dave were both leaning over the man, who was struggling to sit up all the way, and either laughing or crying, she couldn't tell.

The nurse snatched them out of her hands and swiftly attached one of the patient's arms to the metal rails of the gurney.

"You don't want to make me do the other one too, buddy." Dave was breathing hard.

The man twisted and turned like an eel on the narrow mattress, his face contorted savagely. He was younger than she'd first thought. Early thirties, perhaps.

And that awful shoulder.

Maddie put a hand to her own chest, remembering the bright, vicious pain that had gone all the way from her toes to her knee. At least with an ankle, she could hold it totally still.

Whatever was wrong with this guy's arm, he was feeling it every time he moved. Every time he took a breath. She imagining bones grinding against each other, the sound it would make. The damage it would cause.

"You poor thing," she murmured.

She stepped closer to the man, staying out of Jack and Dave's way, and put her palm on his bloodied forehead, the way her mom always did when she was sick.

Mick froze, went silent. His skin was hot and rough, stretched tight over strong bones, hard as sunbaked concrete. He didn't pull away, so she maintained the contact, featherlight and steady.

Then he gasped, like a man bursting out of a cold, dark lake, starved for oxygen. A low, shuddering, keening sound replaced his cries. No crazed laughter, no curses, no fighting, no words at all.

Just that wrenching, awful sound that made her want to take him in her arms and hold him.

"Angel." Mick's face contorted as he cried out and Maddie's heart broke wide open.

"Don't they train volunteers in universal precautions?" Dave elbowed her away from the man and shoved a box of latex gloves at her. "Go. Scrub. No touching without these."

Oops.

She walked to the sink and turned on the tap, fighting dizziness as rust-colored stains swirled off her skin and down the drain, recalling the volunteer coordinator's words when she'd handed Maddie her assignment for the evening.

"We really need the help but it's a busy place. Think you can handle it?" It had been a reasonable question, but also a challenge.

Maddie had assured her she could handle it, but that was the thing about small towns; reputations got set in stone early. Overly high expectations had never been her burden.

Now, taking deep, even breaths through her nose, she looked at the patient in front of her, and wondered why she hadn't offered her time to a nice, clean, blood-free charity.

Like, say, the heritage society. Or the animal shelter

where she'd gotten Clementine. Happy little kittens and puppies.

Not big, rangy bush pilots who weren't cowboys or stockbrokers and made her knees wobble as if the world was tilting.

"You good to take it from here?" Dr. Gallagher straightened up, turning his attention to the old lady in the wheelchair.

Dave nodded. "Go."

Thank God.

Maddie took a step backward.

"Not you," Dave said, a plastic needle cap between his teeth. "Give me that package. I need to start an IV. Distract him."

The man on the gurney jerked. He turned his head toward Maddie and their eyes met again. Her heart stuttered at the wildness, the torment she glimpsed.

"Hang tight, buddy, it'll be okay," Dave said. "Maddie? You're not here for decoration. If you're gloved up now, do whatever you did before."

While Dave gathered gauze and alcohol and whatnot, she stepped to the man's head once more. His tortured gaze, like a bird trapped inside a house, fluttered over hers, then landed. She put her hand alongside his cheek this time. A caress, stunted by latex, like new lovers, not ready to trust.

He blinked, grew still. His breath rasped in his throat but he kept his gaze on hers.

"Sweet angel," he whispered to her.

Oh mercy.

Maddie gulped, unable to look away.

"Keep it up," Dave said. "Almost done."

She took a deep breath, forced herself to smile. "That's better," she murmured. "Stay calm and they'll have you fixed up in no time. It's okay. You're going to be okay. I'm here."

Mick's blue eyes glistened, wide and white-rimmed. His breath came in short, sharp gasps. Then his lids drooped and the rigid muscles in his jaw relaxed.

"There." Dave exhaled, puffing out his cheeks. He stood up and adjusted the clear tubing that ran up to a bag of fluids hanging from the metal pole. "Good job. You're more useful than one might expect. Your resolutions must be sticking."

Maddie sighed. "You were at Grey's on New Year's."

Of course he was.

"So, new and improved Maddie Cash," Dave said, "Mick seems taken with you. Consider him your assignment for the evening."

Mick Meyer opened his eyes fully again, then lifted his head, grimaced – and threw up on Maddie's brand new shoes.

GROUNDED.

Mick Meyer let his head fall back against the crunchy pillow, the ER doc's pronouncement adding to the swirling nausea that confirmed he'd rung his bell but good.

"No flying until further notice." The doctor reiterated the point as if he expected Mick to argue. "Brain injury isn't something to fool around with."

His forehead tingled. He went to lift his hand but found he couldn't. So weak. Too heavy.

"Sorry about that," the doctor said. "You were not what I'd call an ideal patient. I'll take it off, if you promise to stay calm."

Restraints. He'd been fighting. So much pain.

"Yeah. What happened? Was someone... here?"

A girl. Woman. With cool hands. So good.

His arm free now, Mick touched his forehead. There. She'd touched him there.

A song from his childhood drifted into his mind.

Head and shoulders,
Knees and toes,
Knees and toes,
Knees and toes...

His grey matter felt like porridge.

He wiggled his toes. Check. The piggies, at least, weren't squealing.

That made one part of him that was okay.

Oh, he was royally messed up.

"Concussion," Mick said, keeping his eyes closed. "You said mild concussion."

He felt like he'd fallen into a cement mixer.

"Still a brain injury." The doc used a *don't be an idiot* tone. "But you've trashed your shoulder, too. Sprained your knee as well, though you might have done that trying to kick yourself off the gurney."

"Trashed?" His voice sounded like it was coming from the end of a long tunnel. "Issat a technical term?"

"Yup," the doc said. "Dislocated. We're going to put it back in place it as soon as we've ruled out a fracture. We can't put you under so it won't be fun. But it'll be fast, I promise. Dave here will get you ready. You're going to hate him."

Mick opened his eyes as the doctor passed the chart to another man in the doorway and strode off to his next patient.

"I'm Dave, you probably don't remember, but I'll be your torturer tonight." The nurse smiled. "I hear you crashed your plane. You're in pretty good shape, considering."

Mick winced. He hadn't crashed. He'd never crashed. He'd been flying for twelve years and he had a perfect record.

Besides, a crash would have killed him. Wouldn't it?

"I didn't crash."

"Your friends say otherwise. They're waiting outside, pretty persistent."

Beer. Snowmobiles. Laughter. Fish frying on a cast-iron skillet.

Chad's stag. The memory brought a rush of relief.

"Can I see them?"

Dave poked his head out the door. "One of you can come in. Five minutes, that's it. He's got a full dance card tonight. Whew, you've been living rough, haven't you?"

A chorus of *hey, buddy* and *nice going* and *way to cap off a guys' getaway* sounded through the door, setting off fireworks inside his skull. He tried to put names to voices, without success.

Chad jostled Mick's good shoulder. "You look like crap, man."

"I feel fantastic." Mick tucked his bad arm tightly against his belly. The overhead lights had a particularly piercing quality. "You guys totally overreacted."

"Logan's kicking himself that he didn't get it on video. YouTube woulda loved it."

Mick forced himself to concentrate. A minute later, his memory bank creaked open. Logan. Construction guy. Was gonna help fix up Edge's lodge.

"Not many pilots can brag they nearly hit themselves with their own plane," Chad said.

"Glad you enjoyed it." Mick tried to smile. "I'm here all week, folks."

Or more, according to the doc.

"Eric said the slip and fall would have been the real YouTube winner."

Chad's brother? He scraped the inside of his brain pan. Yes. Mick had given Eric the idea to hold Chad's bachelor party at the fishing lodge. He'd been scheduled to fly in from Alaska to check out the place anyway. Two birds, one stone.

They'd had a great time. Until tonight when Mick fired up the Cessna, merely to move it a few hundred yards to protect it from the wind. He wasn't even sure what happened, except that he landed on his head.

"No need to thank us for saving your life," Chad said. "You'd have done the same thing. You know. If you were as tough as us. And could walk and chew gum at the same time."

"Betcha didn't know I could do cartwheels." Talking was almost as much work as thinking.

"That wasn't a cartwheel. That was a cry for help. Freaked out Oz, that's for sure."

"Oz?" How many guys had been there?

"Yeah. Austin." Chad frowned. "You know, the guy who lives on the ranch next door? Bee farmer."

Nothing.

"Under the circumstances," Mick said, pretending he wasn't panicking inside, "I handled that plane pretty damn nicely."

"Eric gave you a solid eight out of ten. Docked you two points on account of botching the dismount." Chad wrinkled his nose. "By the way, we're calling it a crash for the sake of your pride because a parking accident? Buddy, that's just lame."

Mick couldn't argue with that. "Is my plane okay?"

"I don't know. It looked like a rock caught one of the tires."

She was a tough little bird but shit happened. Scenes flickered across Mick's mind like fractured movie frames. His friends, taking turns helping him limp across the frozen lake to the cabin. Packing him into the truck. Carrying him into the ER.

Mick went to lift his hand to his face, but a slicing pain lanced through his shoulder. An aura of rotting garbage drifted in, tightening his gut momentarily.

"You don't want to do that." Chad shook his head grimly. "It's dislocated."

Right. Dislocated.

Trashed.

His head hurt like a son-of-a-bitch and he wished that woman with the cool hands would come and send Chad away. He was so, so tired.

"I need to get outta here," he said. Or thought he said. Chad's voice was so much louder than his.

He had to fix the plane. He had a month to work on the lodge. After that, he had charters lined up from here to Alaska.

Cold sweat broke out over his body. Had the light gotten brighter? Was the room moving?

The nurse came back into the room. "Visit's up. They're ready for him in Imaging."

Mick gulped with relief. His throat wasn't working right.

Too much sound, too much brightness, too much smell.

Too much everything.

He just wanted to be alone. To sleep. And he really, really didn't want to puke. Again.

A beautiful, horrified face. Soft, cool hands on his brow. The sweet whiff of chocolate.

The stench of rot dissipated.

"Thanks. Tell the guys thanks, too," Mick said.

But Chad didn't seem to hear him.

Another nudge, this time on his leg, sent a wave of pain shooting through Mick. Perspiration trickled down his temple. The antiseptic hospital odors overtook the essence of cocoa and turned his stomach. His eyes felt like they were being stabbed with icicles.

He tasted bile at the back of his throat. His face felt hot and his extremities tingled.

"Hey, buddy?" Chad leaned in. Too loud. Too close. "Get better, you hear?"

Mick tried to nod but a muscle in his neck spasmed.

"Staff is staying for a bit. Maddie will keep him posted on how you're doing," Chad added.

Staff? Maddie? Was he supposed to recognize these names?

Cool fingers, breath scented with chocolate.

Mick's head throbbed.

"Yeah, yeah, you love him, he gets it," Dave said, shooing him out. "He's about to toss his cookies. You don't want to be here for that."

Just in time. Mick's stomach clenched. No one wanted to be here for this, including him.

"Here." Dave pressed an emesis basin into Mick's hand. "Common side effect of concussion. You'll feel better soon."

But ten hellacious minutes later, Mick's head still felt like it was going to explode. He needed those cool, soft fingers.

"Liar," he rasped.

"Only when necessary," Dave said. "You won't remember anyway, come tomorrow."

He hit the button on the blood pressure monitor and the cuff inflated, squeezing his good arm. Even that hurt.

"Promise?"

"Sure," Dave said.

Finally, it was quiet. Blissful oblivion called and he followed.

His bed jostled, pulling him back.

"Uh-uh-uh," Dave said, "no sleeping. It's test time. No studying required."

"I hate you."

"I get that a lot," the nurse said.

Chapter Three

MADDIE GLANCED AT her cell phone, then double-checked. Surely it was later than that.

She slipped the phone back into her pocket and assessed herself in the bathroom mirror. Considering she'd done next to nothing and helped next to no one, it had been a traumatic couple of hours. Luckily for her, poor Mick Meyer's stomach had been as empty as the bedpan he'd thrown earlier.

She'd seen tears in his eyes as he'd clung to the bed rail with his good hand. How did doctors and nurses handle being around so much misery all day long?

She walked out of the ladies' room into the hallway, nearly colliding with Logan Stafford.

"Maddie, hey. Chad said you were with Mick. How's he doing?"

"They're about to fix his arm." She went up to give him a hug, then pulled back. "Is it mandatory for men to return from hunting trips reeking like this? That's cancel-the-wedding nasty."

"Ice-fishing, not hunting."

"Hunting, fishing, whatever. Where are the other guys?"

"I sent them home. Storm's blowing up pretty good out there. I was going to hang around a little longer but Samara just called. A couple of trees blew over at Judge Kingsley's place and there's debris blocking the road. My chainsaw's in the truck so I'm going to head over. I don't want to leave Mick, but…"

He left the sentence hanging.

"Go," Maddie said. "I'll keep you posted."

Unlike his rancher friends, Logan lived in Marietta proper in a sweet, little heritage house he'd gutted and restored for Samara and her daughter from a previous marriage. Insta-family, and it fit him like a glove.

Tod had closed that deal. Considered it a waste of time, given the discounted commission.

Maddie wished Logan's current project was further along. Another charitable venture, the deal still wouldn't net her much, but a discounted commission was better than no commission.

A bellowing shriek came from the direction of the emergency room, then cut off abruptly.

Logan winced. "Poor bastard."

Maddie shuddered.

Jack Gallagher came out of the ER and walked toward them.

"Doc," Logan said, "we heard the yelling. Was that

Mick?"

The public address system dinged, calling all available staff to the emergency bay.

"Yeah, we just treated his dislocated shoulder." Jack rubbed the back of his hand across his forehead. He had bags under his eyes. "Should heal nicely. He's a lucky guy. X-ray shows a small hairline fracture in his cheekbone but the rest of his skull is okay. He's waiting on a CT scan. As soon as a bed's ready for him, we're admitting him. The danger now is that he'll fall asleep and slip into a coma. He needs to stay awake. I'm glad you're here, Staff. We're swamped tonight and we need someone to stay with him."

Logan looked torn. Maddie put her hand on his arm.

"Logan's got to go, but I can sit with Mick."

Clementine would be unhappy, but tomorrow, Maddie would let her pounce around in the fresh snow, and all would be forgiven.

"Thanks, Maddie." Jack gave them a tired smile and turned back to the ER.

"You're awesome." Logan squeezed her hand. "Call me if anything else happens, okay?"

"Absolutely." No wonder people got hooked on volunteering. It felt good to do good.

It felt good to be appreciated.

After Logan left, she straightened her shoulders and returned to the curtained area where they'd last put Mick. Would he remember her? He'd been pretty out of it.

"Hey. How's the arm?"

"Fantastic," he said, without moving. "You're not Dave."

A nice, nice voice, despite the gravel of pain.

"That's true, I'm not. I'm Maddie."

His eyes opened, just a slit. Dark blue, narrow, piercing. "Maddie?"

"Yeah. You threw up on my shoes a while ago."

"Did not."

"Well. You tried. I heard your song."

"My song?"

"Head and shoulders, knees and toes." She sang the ditty. "It's familiar but I can't remember from where. Kindergarten?"

"Maybe." He sighed and closed his eyes again. "It's morphine time at the zoo. Be a doll and find my keeper, will you?"

"I'm not a doll," she said. "I'm your volunteer. Maddie. Madeleine. Cash. I'm a friend of Chad's. He's marrying my stepsister? Any of this ring a bell?"

"Congratulations."

But she'd seen something flicker over his face at the mention of her name.

She took a cloth from a stack beside the sink and dampened it with warm water.

"You're Mick Meyer, the pilot. I hear you crashed your plane."

Someone had cleaned the blood off his face, but she ran

the cloth gently over his undamaged skin anyway.

The lines on his brow deepened but he didn't pull away. "Didn't crash. I never crash."

"Huh," she said. "How'd you get injured, then?"

He clicked the call button pinned to his sheet. "Is this thing broken?"

"It's a busy night." Maddie pulled up a chair and sat down next to him. "I'm pinch hitting for Dave. Can you tell me what year it is, Mick?"

She wasn't sure how to talk to someone with a concussion.

"You smell good." A brief smile touched his lips. "Like… like chocolate."

She touched her pocket. "Your nose works, at least. That must be a good sign."

She stroked his hair, gently fingering through the crusted blood. A soft moan escaped his lips.

"Anyone ever tell you," he said, pausing for breath, "you've got boundary issues?"

"I'm a twin. Comes with the territory. How about you?"

"Not a twin. Where is it?"

"Where's what?"

"The chocolate."

She hesitated. Dave hadn't said not to feed him. "It's my emergency stash."

"I'd say this counts. Just one bite. Be an angel."

Angel.

Another flicker of confusion.

She'd heard that concussion was like a hangover, times a million. Poor soul.

"It might make you sick."

"Or it'll cure me."

What the heck. She opened the bag. "It's pretty amazing stuff. The richest, smoothest caramels, covered in dark chocolate, sprinkled with pink Himalayan salt. It's my favorite. Just one bite, then."

He turned his head on the pillow and opened his mouth and she placed the morsel against his teeth. He bit down slowly, carefully.

"Mm." He moaned and, for a moment, the lines in his forehead disappeared.

"Pretty amazing, huh?"

She watched as his mouth worked, his cheeks sucking in slightly, his strong jaw flexing. He seemed transported. She knew how it felt.

She surveyed the remainder of the caramel, the edges scored by his teeth. Her mouth watered. She couldn't put it back in the bag. But she probably shouldn't let Mick have the whole thing. It was so rich.

"Eat it," Mick said.

She started, nearly dropping it. "Oh, no," she said, with a laugh. "I'll leave it here. You can finish it later."

He frowned. "You don't like chocolate?"

"Oh! That's not it. It's just. Well. I gave up chocolate."

His huff of laughter turned into a wince. "Why on earth would you do that?"

At that moment, she couldn't say. There seemed no logical reason for it. She inhaled the warm, rich scent on his breath, and the remaining candy sat right there on the night table, the caramel oozing slightly, shiny and soft, onto the paper napkin.

"Not dieting, I hope. 'Cause you don't need to."

Heat flushed through her. He'd barely seen her. How would he know?

"That's kind of you," she said. "But with Christmas and all, I could certainly stand to lose a few pounds. Who can't, right? Not you, though. I didn't mean you. You look… fine."

She clenched her jaw shut.

Just. Stop. Talking.

He snorted lightly, but she couldn't tell if it was in response to her words, or something else. The skin at his temples was white and tight.

"Where are we at," he said, "on the morphine?"

"That's beyond my pay grade," she said. "Hey, now. Stay with me."

"Eat… the chocolate."

His eyes were fluttering shut. There was nothing a body in pain wanted more than to escape into sleep. How terrible to have that need denied.

"Eat it… or I'm sleeping."

"Fine. But you have to watch." She picked up the chocolate. Her mouth watered. She was doing this for him. It didn't count.

She popped it in her mouth.

Lordy. Smooth, sweet, salty, warm, dark perfection flooded her senses.

"Good, huh?" His eyes were heavy, one swollen almost shut. But he was awake.

"Oh, yeah." She rolled the melting caramel over her tongue.

Mick's gaze grew darker and his breath quickened as he continued watching.

"Are you okay?" She licked her lips, then her fingertip.

"Better than okay," he murmured. "I could watch you eat that all day."

Uh-oh. Boundaries. So not her strong suit.

She searched her mind for another topic of conversation.

"My sister's name is Deirdre. DeeDee. We're fraternal, not identical, so you'll have no trouble telling us apart. She's the 'pretty' one. I'm the 'nice' one." She made air quotes around the words, even though he wasn't looking.

"That's crap," said Mick. "A nice girl would get me drugs."

He sounded remarkably lucid, under the circumstances.

"Drugs will put you to sleep," Maddie said, "and if you sleep, you might not wake up. So I'm being extremely nice, under the circumstances. And my twin is a model. It's kind of definitive."

"Definitive crap." He shifted on the bed, in obvious discomfort. "But you're not pretty, either."

"Huh," she said, stung.

"You're beautiful."

She blinked. He'd said it not as a compliment, but a matter-of-fact statement, without sentiment or ulterior motive.

"Staff," he said suddenly. "Logan Stafford."

Mick sighed, as if he'd just received the answer to one of life's greatest questions. So much for lucid.

"Oh, dear. No, honey, it's me, Maddie. Logan had to go home." He sounded so confused. She got up and peered around the curtain but Dave was nowhere in sight.

Mick lifted one hand, touched the opposite shoulder, his face contorting.

"He's a friend." He pressed his thumb and forefinger against his eyebrows, hard enough to move the flesh, then flinching when he found the cut. Maddie had experienced migraines as a teenager; she suspected he was going through something similar.

"They all are. But the roads are a mess, and Logan needed to go clear some downed trees, so I told him I'd stay with you, instead." She nudged his hand. "You listening?"

"Sure." He squinted at her. "Let me sleep and I'll give you an airplane. Slightly used."

"Slightly crashed, you mean."

He grunted. "No. Crash."

"How's this for a deal? Stay awake and talk to me, and I'll massage your head."

He groaned. "Who are you, exactly? Why are you here?"

"Wow, your short-term memory is wrecked, isn't it? Maddie. Mad. Dee. Lie back."

He let his hand drop back onto the sheet and exhaled heavily. "Volunteer. Right."

She scooted her chair closer, and leaned her elbow on the mattress next to him. "So, Mick Meyer, if you didn't crash your plane, how'd you end up in this bed?"

Very gently, she touched his forehead. He gasped and immediately, she withdrew her hand.

"Did I hurt you?"

"No." The word came out softly, on a breath of air. "Don't... stop..."

There was a kind of quiet desperation in his voice but she wasn't sure if it meant she should stop, or continue.

"Please," he added in a whisper. "You touch... like an angel."

Oh.

His lips were chapped, his skin rough and ruddy and he could use a shower and shave, but again came that overwhelming urge to gather him in her arms and hold him close. He appeared so vulnerable, so alone in his little curtained cubicle, with only her to comfort him.

She pulled her hand away. Mick whimpered, and

clutched her fingers, pressing them first to his lips, then back against his head.

"Please."

Birds fluttered and squawked inside the cage of her chest.

You're in trouble, you're in trouble, you're in trouble.

Big trouble.

The volunteer handbook had mentioned the attachment that sometimes developed between caregivers and those in need. It was a natural response, born of urgency. A kind of survivor bond. Intense, but fleeting.

Not real.

"Hey, Maddie." Dave pulled back the curtain and strode to Mick's side.

Maddie stepped away from the bed, shaking her head.

"How're you doing, Mick?" Dave said, activating the blood pressure machine.

"Kill me," Mick said.

"Hang in there. You'll feel differently tomorrow." He reached for the curtain again. "I need to examine him, Maddie. Give us a minute?"

"Yeah, yes," she stammered. "Of course. I'll go... pee. Or something."

But instead of heading to the ladies' room, she pushed open the door to the stairwell, and sank to the top step. She was used to the fun of flirting, the rush of attraction, the novelty, the challenge.

The game.

But this odd intimacy that had sprung up between her and Mick didn't feel like a game. It didn't feel like some kind of normal, transient, emergency room attachment, either.

It felt... bigger.

Maddie dropped her head in her hands with a groan. "No, no, no. Not now."

She was off men. Taking a break from the whole scene. She did not need the distraction of another crush.

Especially one that felt... big.

"Listen to yourself," she muttered, thumping her head gently against the concrete wall beneath the hand rail.

Maybe if they had time, they could scan *her* brain, too.

She got back to her feet. She would find someone else to watch over Mick, apologize to Dave – that would be fun – say goodbye and good luck. Then she'd go home and curl up with Clementine and a handful of jellybeans and research ways to give back to the community that didn't involve bodily fluids.

Or complicated... reactions.

She could do that. She would do that.

When she returned to the ER, she found Dave outside Mick's cubicle, jotting notes onto a clip board.

"Good, you're back," Dave said. "He's asking for you."

"Angel!" Mick called from behind the curtain. "Where's my chocolate?" The strident, panicky note was back.

"Don't worry," Dave said. "It's the concussion talking. But he's a lot calmer with you. How long can you stay?"

Maddie glanced at the curtain. She was either a coward or a saint.

Cancel saint. Try idiot.

"I'm not qualified for this, Dave." It was a lame excuse.

"You're qualified to babysit, aren't you? That's all this guy needs. Just until HR sends me another pair of hands."

"Dave!" Jack Gallagher called from another cubicle somewhere. "We need you in here."

"Coming," Dave said. "Maddie. We're taking him up to a room shortly. Just stay with him for a little longer, okay? Sit. Chat. You'll be fine."

Maddie watched him go, leaving her trapped, pulled in, sucked under and way, way out of her depth.

In those long nights last spring when she'd huddled with Cynthia and Mom and DeeDee over Norman's bed in the cardiac care ward, she'd found herself praying, begging, promising that if only her stepdad would pull through, she'd change her ways, become someone responsible, reliable, mature.

Someone that might inspire the same pride she heard when he spoke about Cynthia.

Norm had made it. So Maddie kept her promise. She passed her licensing exam. She got hired at Styles Realty. She got her own apartment, dusted off the treadmill, learned to make kale chips. Quit shopping the cowboy market at Grey's every Friday night. Started volunteering. She even adopted a dog!

Notwithstanding her little fall from grace on New Year's Eve, and, well, the little issue of her job, she was doing it. She was being responsible, reliable, and mature, as promised.

Mick wasn't in his right mind, but she was. It was up to her to keep things in line.

She took a breath and turned back to Mick's curtained cubicle.

She could do this. She refused to let her wild imagination ruin what was left of her fresh start.

But the moment she walked back into the room, the man in the bed croaked, "Angel. Thank God."

And the birds in her chest revived their raucous chorus.

THE ONE GOOD thing about Mick's head hurting so freaking much was that he didn't even think about his shoulder or his knee. Until he moved, at least.

Even then, the pain from his limbs seemed to radiate straight up into eye, his skull, his cheekbone pulsing and throbbing with every beat of his heart, as if his brain was raw, exposed to the open air. And on fire.

Until she'd touched him.

He shifted on the stiff sheets and with his good hand, pointed to his forehead. "Please," he said. Only it came out sounding more like nails on a chalkboard. He cleared his throat. "It helped. When you touched me."

The girl – woman – crossed her arms and remained

standing. Maddie. Peering cautiously into the already dimly lit room, he could see that she really was an angel. She wore something blue, soft and shapeless. A tight honey-blonde bun of hair, scrubbed skin that shone like silk and eyes so bright and warm and innocent. What hid beneath that ugly top? Curves that could bring a man to his knees, he guessed.

Assuming he was standing to begin with.

"I don't bite," he added.

"You do smell though."

He tried to grin. Failed. "You offering a bed bath?"

"And you said I had boundary issues." But there was a smile in her voice. She pulled the chair closer to his bed and sat down next to him again. "Don't get any ideas."

"Current condition... notwithstanding," Mick said, "I'm a man. Men always have... ideas."

The words squeezed out like drops from a damp sponge but it was worth it. He was still able to flirt. After nearly offing himself out of sheer stupidity. Well, it was good to know his libido wasn't damaged.

Not that he could do anything about it.

"Don't worry," he said. "I'm a lame duck. Sprained knee, dislocated wing. Not to mention the noggin. Which is killing me, by the way. Could be... the concussion, but it appears you... have a halo. Angels are sweet and merciful, so, not to beg, but... I'm begging. Since you're here."

Mick had enjoyed his share of female companionship over the years. Unlike his pals, his heart had never been snared, leaving him free to take to the air whenever he wanted, for whatever job sounded interesting.

Women tended to want men with stuff. Prospects. A future. The only thing he owned was his Cessna, a tidy stock portfolio and the clothes on his back. So it worked.

"I am here," she said. And touched him.

"Ahh." Wetness trickled down his temples and she brushed it away. That eye, the throbbing one, was swollen and tight, leaking. Tears? Was he crying? Or was it oozing blood? Probably not blood. People tended to freak out about blood.

She set an ice pack at the back of his neck, and wrapped another around his knee.

"Cold," he said, shivering.

"I know. Sorry." Her fingers pressed and kneaded, painful, but a different kind of pain than the headache. A better pain. Like a good pain was fighting to destroy the bad pain.

An epic battle, inside his skull, with him as spectator and gladiator at once.

"So, your uncle has a fishing lodge."

The words nudged him out of the arena, back into the room.

"Sorry," Maddie said. "No sleeping, remember?"

Damn. A thought worked its way through the murk. What had she asked?

The lodge. A funeral. Property transfer. Taxes… Right.

"My uncle," he said. "Edge. Reg, actually. He hated that

name."

Crazy Uncle Edge's chunk of wilderness that no one wanted to deal with.

"It's his cabin?" Maddie's fingers worked through his hair, pulling and teasing lightly. He swore he could feel nerves sizzling down to the very last fiber.

"It is. Was. He's dead. Died."

"I'm sorry."

The whole reason he and his buddies had chosen that particular remote area of Montana's Gallatin Range for their getaway in the first place. He now owned it. Or half, at least.

The stress of the past few weeks came rushing back. He'd promised his mother he'd sell the property as quickly as possible. Charlene hadn't known Edge had named her as beneficiary, had barely talked with her brother in the past several years. To get a letter saying he'd passed away had devastated her. She'd always hoped that one day they'd be close again.

"Good guy, Edge." It came out goo-gye-esh. "Looked after m'mom."

"Family is important. Do you have brothers and sisters, Mick?"

He began to shake his head. Before he could, she stilled him with her fingers but even that subtle intention set his eye, the whole side of his head pounding again.

"Just me and mom."

He wanted to sleep, so badly. But he also wanted to stay

in this wonderful, starlit, twilight zone where the real world was a curtain away and it was just him and Maddie and she kept touching him, touching him.

"You're close," she said. "You and your mom. That's nice."

Were they close? He'd been on the move since he'd started flying, never in one place for more than a few months at a time. He checked in with her regularly though. Often enough?

"She's a waitress. In Billings." He was slurring. "Edge left her everything. He's a good brother. Was. He was."

It turned out Edge had money squirrelled away in accounts all over the world. For a quiet small-town woman used to the rigors of single motherhood, it was overwhelming. Mick was naturally helping her with it all, but this piece of land, unaccountably left to them both, was an obvious thing he could take off her hands. The sooner Edge's estate was settled, the sooner Charlene could properly process his death, and begin getting back to her life.

Mick was touched that Edge had left Charlene the means to live out her life free of financial worry. But he wished the man had prepared her for it, or at least kept in touch.

He turned his head and an icepick of pure agony stabbed through his eye to the base of his skull.

"Hey, hey," came a soft voice, "whatever you're doing, stop it."

Suddenly the featherlight drift of soft fingertips slipped

down to his neck, across to his shoulder. She pulled the ice pack away and he inhaled sharply, as a fresh set of gladiators entered the arena.

"Good?" Maddie whispered the word, trailing her finger over his eyebrows, down into the bones around his eyes, massaging gently upward along his temples.

"Oh." Mick moaned. "Yes."

All the family stress and sadness evaporated, fizzled into the healing tidal rush that ran along his nerve endings.

"Good. Let me know if I do anything to hurt you, okay?"

He moaned again. "I knew you were an angel of mercy. Marry me."

Her fingers froze and he heard her quick intake of air.

"Joke, Maddie. Kidding. Woman like you. Probably married your high school sweetheart. Eight rug rats tearing up the town. Yeah?"

She smiled at that, he was relieved to see.

"No. I don't. I didn't. I mean, I'm single."

"Ah." He groaned as she moved her fingers more firmly, massaging in small circles around to his hairline. "In that case, let's set a date. I can't live without you."

The numerous sounds around them, quick footsteps, clattering metal meal trays, dinging elevators, and rapid-fire conversations felt like hail on a tin roof. But Maddie's laughter landed softly, tinkling on his eardrums like a gentle rain.

"I don't know," she said. "I'm looking for a turnkey operation. You're more of a fixer-upper."

"Harsh but true." He paused. "Wait. I've got an old fishing lodge and a few acres of weedy lakefront. Does that sweeten the deal?"

Her fingers stilled and the pressure lessened. He cracked open his eyes. She had an odd expression on her face.

"Sorry, pass. I've heard about your roach motel."

Women and stuff. It was just a game, but he felt disappointed anyway.

"What?" she said. "Just because I like to sleep vermin-free doesn't mean I'm not tough."

"Sure," he said. "The manicure was a dead giveaway."

She laughed in protest and her fingers began moving again.

"Okay, I was pretty spoiled as a kid but I'm making my own way in the big, bad world now. Have you heard of this thing called rent? It's really inconvenient."

He could hear the smile in her voice and his own lips lifted in response. It didn't hurt. "I hear mortgages are even worse."

The rhythmic press and slide of her hands had a hypnotic effect on him, lulling and easing like the ebb and flow of tidewater on a tropical beach.

"See? We've got something in common, after all," Maddie said. She kept her voice low. "We could run away and be broke and free together. See the world."

He'd already seen the world and he was nowhere near broke. But he'd gladly spend his last dime to show it to Maddie.

It felt like the world outside his room, outside this little cubicle in which his bed and Maddie's chair sat, had receded to some other dimension. This was a space outside of ordinary time, suspended and removed like a picture cut from a photo album.

The two of them strangers, yet thrown together for these few hours, so momentous for Mick in his pain and, yes, he'd admit it, his fear.

What was it for Maddie? Just another evening spent at the bedside of a needy hospital patient?

He understood how concussions worked. Tomorrow, he could wake up – assuming he was eventually allowed to sleep – with no recollection of this conversation, or the touch of her magic hands. Or their gentle flirting, the ease with which they joked about their lives.

He lifted his hand and grasped her wrist, lightly. She stilled. Their eyes met, hers wide and dark, questioning but unalarmed.

"Mick?"

Perhaps he'd be left with a fleeting, dream-like vision of a woman with soft hands and a kind voice. An angel.

Or perhaps he'd see her again and she'd be a complete stranger to him.

"Kiss me?" he whispered.

"Mick." She pulled her hand, but he didn't let it go.

"I know it's not real, Maddie," he said. "In an hour or two you'll go home."

"And come morning, you'll probably forget we ever met."

Understanding filled her dark eyes, warm and sad.

"I don't want to forget you, Maddie."

"But you will. And it's okay."

"So, kiss me. Maybe I won't."

She smiled at him, so sweetly he could already taste her lips on his.

Strawberries? Chocolate? Pancakes and syrup? He had to know.

But she touched a finger to his lips.

"Like you said, this isn't real. It's adrenalin and pain and endorphins and whatever they're pumping into you through that IV drip."

"Right now, it's real."

She leaned closer.

"I'm eighty percent certain that this isn't allowed. Maybe ninety."

"Do it for me."

She bent forward, very slowly, keeping her gaze on his, holding his hand. He inhaled a trace of something light and flowery, lotion perhaps. Or her shampoo. It smelled... purple. Like lilac.

Remember this. Keep this.

Light shone behind her head, renewing the halo he'd seen earlier. A lock of golden hair slipped free of the pins, fell over her shoulder and brushed against his cheek. Her neck was fragrant as a garden warmed by the sun.

Lilac, spring breeze, sunshine.

Ever so lightly, like the first touch of floats on a glassy lake, she pressed her hands to his face, her lips to his.

And then they were gone, leaving a cool spot on his skin.

He tucked the memories into his brain, like petals in a book, even knowing the book would get filed away in a locked library, the key to which lay beneath the frozen surface of a lost lake.

Hold on. Hold this.

Lilacs. Sunshine. Love.

"I have to go," she whispered.

"No."

"By tomorrow, you'll have forgotten all about me."

Hold on.

Footsteps approached. Another voice. The rattle of wheels and metal.

"You will forget." Maddie put her face next to his ear. Her breath warmed his cheek. "But I won't."

And then she was gone.

Chapter Four

AS SHE PUT the last pin in her hair before leaving for work, Maddie had almost convinced herself that she was glad Mick Meyer wouldn't remember what had occurred between them that evening in the emergency room. She was questioning her own recall of the events, in fact.

Another impulsive decision. Another regrettable kiss.

What was it with her lips?

"At least this time there were no witnesses," she said to Clementine, scooping the little dog into her designer carrier, the blue and green plaid playing nicely off her own teal coat. Elinor had graciously allowed Maddie to bring Clem to work with her from time to time.

As in, all the time. Clem made people smile.

Maybe she should take her visiting at the hospital. They'd taken the course and Clem had passed all her tests. There were lots of sick people who could use a smile, right?

As Maddie pulled her car up in front of the Java Cafe, the brisk January air caught in her lungs and made a lacy breath cloud around her face.

"Guard the car, baby," she instructed, before beeping the lock shut.

A little peace offering. Good will to men. And women. And especially bosses.

Given her probation and all.

Focus on work, Maddie.

Start the day, the month – the year – off right. She had to snag a sale and soon. She should have kept the commission on Rosie Linn's house. No! She'd made the right decision. She wouldn't have been able to live with herself if she'd profited from a sale between two people who were almost spouses.

She put her order in and while she waited for it to be filled, she told herself to stop thinking about Mick Meyer.

She put her beverages into a cardboard travel tray.

"Thanks, hon," she called, leaving a tip in the employee therapy jar.

She set the tray on the floor of her car and carefully drove the last block to work.

With that nasty wound on his cheek and eyebrow, Mick was lucky his eye wasn't damaged. He'd probably end up with a scar, but on someone like him, it would just add to his charm.

No.

No charm.

No thinking about him. She'd overstepped her position as a volunteer by about a mile. It was a huge mistake and she was just lucky that she hadn't gotten caught.

But there was nothing wrong with checking up on him, was there? He was a family friend, after all.

She pushed open the doors to Styles Realty with her butt, balancing the take-out carton of coffees.

"Good morning, Madeleine." Elinor Styles walked into the reception area with a smile. Elegant and put-together, Elinor's easy approachability hid a quick mind and ruthless salesmanship.

She bent down to peer into the plaid carrier. "Hello, Clementine. Aren't you chic today?"

"Black, one sugar," Maddie said, depositing the cup into her boss's waiting hands. "Where's Alisa?"

"Did I hear my name?" The office assistant jogged in from around the corner. "Oh, you brought coffee! Gimme!"

"You call that coffee?" Tod joined them in Elinor's office, dressed GQ perfect as always, even if his too-pink cheeks ruined the effect. "If it's got whipped cream on it, it's dessert."

"If it's got dairy," Alisa shot back, "it's breakfast."

"Happy New Year, Maddie," Tod said, with a smirk. "I see you brought your rat to work with you again."

Ugh. Gummy worms.

"Elinor," Maddie said, "Tod's hitting on me again."

Elinor sighed. "Sometimes I wish he was gay."

Tod's cheeks went from pink to dull red. "Mother!"

Maddie choked on her coffee and Tod turned on his heel

and stormed out.

"What?" Elinor said, as both women burst out laughing. "The son of a college friend of mine just adopted a little girl with his partner. All the grandma perks, without having to deal with a daughter-in-law. It's the perfect situation."

"He does have great fashion sense," Alisa said.

"I'm not gay," Tod called from the other room.

"Plus," continued Elinor, lifting her eyes skyward, "he's gone through half the women in Marietta, and who knows how many more out of town. And none of them were worth bringing home. Except you, Maddie," she added quickly.

Maddie choked mid-laugh. "But we never—"

"Oh, I know, I know, mistletoe, countdown, wrong place, wrong time. I get it." Elinor made a shushing gesture with her hands. "And it would be a disaster if you did get together, anyway. It's just that, well…"

"I'm the nicest girl your son never dated?" Maddie suggested.

"A fair statement," Elinor said.

"Aw." Alisa stared flatly at Maddie. "Isn't that adorable."

Heat crept over Maddie's skin. Alisa had worked at the office far longer than Maddie, and loved everything about the business. The fact that she answered phones, while Maddie held the title of realtor was a sore spot.

Maddie's probation had improved Alisa's temperament considerably.

Maddie kissing the boss's son had not.

Thoughtless words, thoughtless actions, thoughtless kisses. Maddie was the master of regrettable impulses.

Then she thought of that kiss in the emergency room. A kiss she could still feel on her lips. Another one she should regret.

But didn't.

Elinor's expression grew serious. She got up and put her hand on the doorknob. "Alisa, would you mind? I'd like to have a word with Maddie."

Uh-oh.

"No problem." Alisa walked out, giving Maddie a triumphant wave as she passed.

"Sit down, Maddie."

Nerves began quivering, sending the coffee in her stomach sloshing about. "Okay," she said. "But I'm not marrying your son, no matter how much you pay me."

She lowered herself into one of Elinor's stylish but uncomfortable tub chairs, feeling like she was in grade school again, in yet another meeting with the principal.

"You're a delight to have in the office, dear. You're always chipper. Your clients love you. Few women are able to put Tod in his place the way you can, and that's a pure joy."

Elinor didn't smile but her voice was kind.

Too kind.

Maddie lifted Clementine from her carrier and held her against her chest. "I know I need to work harder, Elinor. I'm trying. I just need more time."

She spoke too fast, her voice too high.

Elinor leaned her elbows on her desk and steepled her fingers, tapping the tips together. "So you've said. But let's examine things from a business perspective, shall we?"

She pulled up a spreadsheet on her computer, then swung the monitor around so that they could view it together.

"Here's an overview of Styles Realty since you came on board."

Elinor ran her hand down the lists of clients, sales, open houses, commissions, expenses, all the day-to-day activities involved in selling property.

Maddie's eyes glazed over but one fact was painfully clear—her name was on lots of listings, but almost no completions.

Elinor pointed to a photo of an old listing. "Case in point. The two-story across from the library. You had a buyer, ready to make an offer. And you sent him away."

"It was all wrong for him," Maddie protested. "His elderly mother lives with him. He needed a rancher, something with no stairs. It would have been wrong to sell it to him."

"In your opinion." Elinor looked steadily across her desk. "He bought it anyway. From Tod."

"That poor lady is going to fall and break her hip," said Maddie. "I hope Tod can live with that."

Elinor sighed. "Do you have any active listings right now?"

Maddie could hear the refrigerator in the staff room humming. She turned to the window, watching the people bustling on the street, their heads down against the wind and snow, everyone taken up in their own private worries.

Elinor wouldn't really fire her. Would she?

"I've got a young couple who are looking." A couple with a baby on the way who deserved to have their interests protected. She wouldn't rush them. Not until she'd found the perfect place for them.

"When someone decides to buy or sell property, Maddie, your job is to help them do it, not interfere with their decision. I know you mean well. But it's not your place."

She'd said it herself, hadn't she?

No more meddling.

Maddie swallowed. "You're right. I know you are. And I've changed my ways. See? Neutral colors. No cleavage. I'm really trying, Elinor."

"I know, dear." Elinor exhaled and folded her manicured hands on the desk in front of her. "But, Maddie, real estate is a tough business. And Styles Realty is my company. You are my employee." She pressed her lips together. "It wasn't your call to cancel the Linn contract."

"Oh," Maddie said.

This was bad. It had been an impulse move, but it would have been wrong to take their money. Surely Elinor could see that.

"I know you meant well, Maddie. We won't speak of it

again. However, you need to make up the shortfall. If I let you slide… well." She straightened her shoulders. "You can do this, I know you can. You may have to make sacrifices. Your social life, for instance. Hobbies. Volunteer work. You have to prioritize your job. If you want to keep it."

The buzz of the refrigerator got louder, drowning out Elinor's words.

Hours and hours of training courses. All that time sequestered in her room, on her laptop, learning stuff like listing agreements, contract law, property transfer. Zoning, for goodness sake.

"Maddie?"

She blinked. "Yes. Right. Prioritize. Got it."

"This is your last warning, Maddie."

Years of cautions echoed through her head. *Live up to your potential, Maddie. You can do so much better, Maddie. If only you'd try, Maddie.*

"No more warnings." She nodded like a bobble-head. Clementine licked her chin. "Got it. I can do better, Elinor."

"Find your clients a house. One deal. That's all I ask. If one month isn't enough time, well…" She shrugged apologetically. "I hope it won't come to that."

One month?

All that work, everything she did for her clients, all the mistakes she kept them from making, the hours she put in searching for just the right homes…

Maddie squeezed her eyes shut for a moment. "I can do

it, Elinor."

"I know you can." Her boss lifted her eyebrows, then reached over and patted Maddie's hand. "Thanks for the coffees. Why don't you take some time away from the office to gather your thoughts? Take an early weekend. In fact, take next week too, work from home. Call me when you've got a deal."

Chapter Five

M ADDIE TURNED THE key in the ignition and sat
shivering while the engine warmed up. Winter in
Montana was the definition of frigid, despite the brilliant
sunshine. It was almost insulting, how cheerfully the teasing
light danced over everything in its path, all the brightness
but none of the warmth.

Work from home? With *Friends* reruns and match.com
to distract her? She might as well pack her things and move
back to the ranch right now. She could keep Norm company. Mom would love having someone else to cook for again.

No one expected her to become a real estate mogul, anyway.

A yip sounded from the carrier. Clementine's silky top-
knot quivered and pushed through the opening, then her
head popped up.

"Hey, baby," Maddie said, her throat catching.

She pulled the little doggie out and buried her face in the
soft fur. She was responsible for this tiny creature's well-
being. Without a job, how would she buy dog food?

Clementine depended on her to be the grown-up here and that was that.

"Thank you, honey." She kissed the dog on the nose and then secured her back into the carrier. "Don't tell Grandma about the wallowing, okay?"

She cranked the heater to high and pulled onto Main Street. There was only one place to go at a time like this— Copper Mountain Chocolates. She needed the soothing ambiance and a bracing conversation with a good friend. Also, if anyone in Marietta was planning a move, real-estate-wise, Sage Carrigan would know.

Of course, it would be tempting. And dropping in without buying would be rude. Maddie believed in supporting local business. But she didn't have to buy anything for herself. She'd get a thank you gift for the ER staff, for putting up with her. And the volunteer coordinator, as an apology for quitting. She cringed at the thought.

But, if she was dropping by the hospital anyway, she could bring some caramels for Mick.

That was reasonable, right?

She ignored the frisson of excitement that the thought stirred in her.

Most likely Mick wouldn't remember her. She should be hoping he wouldn't remember her. That kiss. She really shouldn't have done that.

But how could he not remember that kiss? She couldn't forget, and she'd tried.

As soon as she saw the chocolate shop storefront, so cheery and bright, her spirits lifted. She hiked Clem's carrier higher onto her shoulder, pushed open the door and inhaled the sweet, wondrous goodness of Copper Mountain Chocolate air.

Her mouth watered as appetite sucker-punched her. She should have had something more than coffee for breakfast. Sage's famous hot chocolate simmered in the shiny copper pot behind the counter. The gleaming display case mocked her with row after row of sinfully rich confections. Smooth and dark, rich and milky, truffles, nut clusters, champagne caramels and her favorites, the chocolate covered Himalayan pink salt caramels.

She drew the aromas deep into her lungs. Maybe she'd buy a few chocolates for herself after all. Just a small package. For her roadside emergency kit, in case she got stuck in the snow somewhere.

"Not for eating," she muttered to herself. "For an emergency."

No more chocolate.

Maybe she could claim she'd been joking.

She stepped past the display case, craning her head toward the small kitchen at the back of the shop where Marietta's premium delicacies were hand-crafted with only the finest ingredients.

"Hello! I may be having a minor crisis that's making me weak. Whatever you do, don't let me have any chocolate."

She paused. The heady bouquet swirling around the pretty store was enough to break the strongest resolve. "Unless it's Himalayan salt caramels. No! Not even then!"

Sage Carrigan came through the door at the back with a smile and ran her hands over the apron bearing the logo of her business and passion, Copper Mountain Chocolates.

"Breaking your New Year's resolution already? Now, that's what I call a true friend. Though I hope you're being overly dramatic about the crisis." Sage wore her auburn hair in a long braid that showcased her elegant neck and creamy skin.

Maddie groaned and glanced at the ceiling. "Working for a living is harder than I thought."

"Truer words were never spoken." Sage put her arms around Maddie.

It felt so good. Unlike Sage and her sisters, who'd grown up with a stern father, she and DeeDee had lost their dad when they were barely toddlers. Joanie had spent a fortune attempting to fill the void with toys and activities and clothes and vacations. They were, as she'd admitted to Mick, spoiled.

Their stepdad Norm was wonderful, but they'd already been sixteen when he and Joanie got married and even with his then fourteen-year old daughter Cynthia, he was hardly authoritative.

"How can I help?" Sage said.

"You just did. Also, don't let me eat anything. I'm hoping that inhaling will be enough to satisfy my craving."

Portia Bishop, Sage's niece, came from the back room bearing a tray of packaged treats for the display case.

"Hey, Maddie," she said, "how are you doing?"

"Ugh," Maddie said. "More importantly, how are you?"

The girl had lost the pinched expression she'd had when she arrived in autumn, after announcing that she'd quit college and needed a job. But her eyes remained haunted and she was too quiet. Some of the pieces had fallen into place when they realized that she was pregnant, though the fact that she wouldn't talk about the baby, the father, or her future, left most of the puzzle unsolved.

"Fine. You want these here, Sage?"

Sage gave Portia some instructions, then led Maddie to a small table and pushed her gently into a chair.

"So, what's wrong?"

"Elinor sent me home. Says I have to make a sale before the end of the month. Or…"

"Or what?"

Maddie shrugged. "I'd rather not find out."

"That's bad. Did she say why?"

She slumped back against her chair. "I'm having a dry spell. Because I won't show young couples a pretty facade without mentioning the dry rot underneath, because I won't encourage them to borrow beyond their means for a mistake that could ruin them. Because I'm looking out for their best interests. But Elinor says I'm going too far. Apparently I've lost sales to other agents who've been willing to show them places I know they won't be happy with."

"Those agents must love you."

Maddie put her head in her hands. "A lot of people think moving will solve their problems, when what they're really doing is running away. The Logans, from nearby Sweetheart, for instance. They needed marriage counseling. And the Bradners? They needed to adjust to being empty nesters. They used their equity to renovate. Now they get to keep their lovely yard and have the house of their dreams. Without paying a hefty realtor fee."

"And you wonder why Elinor is thinking of letting you go."

"Yeah," Maddie said, "now that I hear it out loud…"

Sage went to the counter, opened a drawer and pulled out a tiny cookie. "Is it okay if I give Clementine a treat? It's hypoallergenic, all vegetable. No chocolate for you, Miss Muffet."

She bent down and unzipped the carrier just enough to give Clementine the treat and a scratch behind the ear. She was such a good friend.

"At least one of us can enjoy a treat here," Maddie said. "Yes, I'm moping. If I can't have chocolate, at least let me enjoy a good mope."

Sage eyed her. "Hang on. I know just the thing."

Maddie bent forward until her head hit the table, and bounced it there lightly, twice.

It hurt. Which made her think of Mick.

She banged her forehead again, a little harder, and closed her eyes. No men was even worse than no chocolate. Or at least, equally bad.

"Whoa," Sage said. "Easy on the table. Here. Guaranteed to cure the winter blahs."

"This is a bit more than the blahs."

"Drink this and it won't be."

Maddie sat up and took the mug her friend held out to her. The rich balm of chocolate and cinnamon and a dollop of gooey whipped cream went straight to her lizard brain, bypassing conscious thought.

No.

She set the mug on the table. "I can't."

"You pledged to give up chocolate," said Sage. "This is hot cocoa. A beverage, not food. It's entirely different. Besides, you shouldn't have promised to quit chocolate in the first place. You make it sound like it's a bad thing. I'm trying not to take it personally."

Maddie looked at the creamy froth. "It's mostly milk, right?"

Sage lifted an eyebrow. "Sure. If it makes you feel better."

"It does." Maddie lowered her lips to the life-giving elixir. It tasted even better than it smelled. The smooth liquid flowed over her tongue and down her throat, loosening the tight knot of fear that had lodged above her heart. It settled in her stomach, warming, soothing.

Guilt-inducing.

She took another sip, then licked the foamy residue that clung to her top lip.

"This is what love tastes like," she said.

Sage laughed. "You must be channeling my new marketing guru. That's exactly what Krista's using for my campaign."

Maddie took another deep gulp. "It's perfect."

"Speaking of marketing." Sage grimaced. "Portia and Rosie are pushing me to hold another event of some kind. January is a dead month, with everyone sticking to their diets. Ahem. No names mentioned. Got any ideas?"

"Hey, I'm one of the no names mentioned."

"They're thinking of a how-to class. You don't have to eat the chocolate. You just have to show up, be your usual friendly, fun self and make us look good. If we run one, will you come? Please?"

"You bet. That's the kind of friend I am." In her mind's eye, she saw Elinor shaking her head. "Unless I have a client meeting, of course."

The bells above the door tinkled as Chad Anders entered the store.

"Two of my favorite ladies, at one time," he said with his trademark grin.

"Hey, Chad. Do you want another hot chocolate, Maddie?" said Sage. "You're welcome to stay, regardless."

Maddie shook her head. "Hey, Chad."

"Looking a little down in the dumps there, sis." He dropped a kiss onto her cheek, then poked his fingers into the carrier to give Clementine a pat.

Sage glanced between them. "Maddie needs to make a sale. Why don't you subdivide a chunk of Anders Run? You'd never miss it. Be a good future brother-in-law."

"I think my actual brother might object," he said. "Maddie, if you need a sale, you should talk to Mick."

Maddie felt her face bloom at the sound of Mick's name. Suddenly, the hot chocolate wasn't the only thing warming her on the inside.

"Who's Mick?" Sage asked.

Chad gave Sage the quick overview of their stag weekend and its unfortunate ending.

"Mick happened to be in the ER when I was volunteering." Maddie grimaced, hoping to derail the conversation. "Which I'm not doing anymore in an effort to stay gainfully employed."

"Well," Sage said, not distracted in the least, "from the look on your face, he made a pretty strong impression."

"Sympathy." Maddie shrugged, aiming for nonchalance. "I felt bad for him. That's all."

"If he impressed you then," Chad said with a chuckle, "you should see him when he's on his game. He wants to sell the fishing lodge we stayed at. Didn't he mention it?"

Her heart sped up. This was a definite reason to visit.

"He mentioned 'a few acres of lakefront' but he wasn't exactly a reliable narrator at the time."

Chad's eyebrows rose. "Try six hundred forty acres, on both sides of the Marietta River."

Maddie blinked. Her hand froze on the handle of the mug, letting it hover halfway to her lips.

"Whoa," Sage said. "That would soften Elinor up."

"His uncle left it to Mick and his mom equally. I'm on my way to visit him right now," Chad said. "Want me to have him call you?"

"Sure!" She caught herself, cleared her throat. "Sure, if you think he's serious. I could do an initial evaluation, at least, give him some options. You know. Real estate wise. Something to talk over. With his mom. Or... whoever."

Subtle. But it occurred to her with sudden horror that she'd kissed the man without knowing whether or not he was free. The banter and flirting and lack of visitors seemed to indicate so, but it was a dangerous assumption.

She fumbled in her bag for a business card and handed it to Chad.

"Here. Give him this. He can call anytime. Or I can see him. In the hospital."

Her forehead was sweating. She gulped the last of her drink.

"Is that hot chocolate?" Chad eyed her mug. "I thought you'd sworn off it."

"It's a soothing milk-based beverage," she said. "Don't

tell Cynthia."

"I see nothing," he said, choosing a small package of chocolate-covered nut clusters from the shelf. "And it's just Mick and his mom. No siblings. Or... whatever."

Chad grinned and set his purchases on the counter. Maddie glanced at Sage, who was also smiling at her in an uncomfortably knowing way.

"What?" she said.

"Either that soothing milk-based beverage cured your crisis, or—"

"What do you know, it's all gone." Maddie tipped her empty mug to her lips and smacked it on the bottom, like a ketchup bottle, then got to her feet. "Clementine and I should be going. People to see, houses to sell."

"I'll tell him to call you." Chad eyed her as he paid for his items. "Though he's not up to making business decisions right now."

"Don't worry," Sage said with a snort. "Maddie's ethical to a fault."

Maddie's heart swelled. Sage the defender.

A slight frown marred Chad's handsome forehead. "Mick's a great guy, Maddie. But he never stays in one place for long. You should know that."

His concern bit deep and whatever little fantasy Maddie had been building, despite herself, shattered.

"Why would that matter to me?" She tucked a strand of hair behind her ear. She could never manage to get it to stay pinned up properly.

"Good." Chad zipped up his jacket. "I know you're not an attaching kind of girl. But I had to warn you anyway. You're almost my sister, after all."

He took his bag and left, letting a rush of cold air into the shop.

She wasn't an *attaching* kind of girl? What did that mean?

"Ignore him," Sage said. "You like this Mick guy, I can tell. So, see where it goes. You never know."

"He's in the hospital! He probably doesn't even remember me. And besides, I'm done with men, remember?" Maddie said, digging through her bag for her wallet. "This is business only."

"Oh, Maddie." Sage gently pushed Maddie's hand away. "The hot chocolate is free, because it comes with advice. Don't ignore a chance for something special because of pride. I know what I'm talking about. Now, go home and study up on recreational property sales."

When Maddie left the store, she barely felt the chilly wind on her face.

That night with Mick had been as far from a date as possible. It certainly hadn't been fun. Yet, it had been the most memorable time she'd spent with a man in ages.

So she'd see him again. As a realtor. There was nothing wrong with that. The ball would be in his court. No undue influence. No meddling.

No advantage-taking.

She'd keep things strictly professional. Okay, so she fed him chocolate. And kissed him. Not the best start to a professional relationship.

But that was her little secret. No one would ever know.

She felt hopeful for the first time since before the holidays. Mick had land to sell. She needed to close a deal. Win-win.

MADDIE SPENT THE rest of the day being responsible. She dropped Clementine off at the groomers for a bath and nail trim. She bought groceries. She got the oil changed in her car. She chickened out of going to the hospital and instead called the volunteer coordinator, who accepted Maddie's resignation with an unsettling lack of surprise.

That was okay. She'd go to the hospital tomorrow, bearing gifts, head held high. That would give Mick another day to recover. Let Chad talk her up first. It wouldn't be fair to bombard him while he was still sick, anyway.

But as she opened her credit card bills while riding the elevator to her floor, she admitted that a little bombarding might be required. Because she was in trouble.

She walked into her apartment and dropped her scarlet Coach bag on the beautiful custom pine hall table she'd commissioned from Chad. The table that matched the bookcase against the wall, the entertainment cabinet and the dining room table that seated six, even though she barely cooked for one.

She'd ordered an apartment full of furniture that cost her a fortune, even with Chad's generous I'm-in-love-with-your-stepsister discount and payment plan, all before she'd received her first pay check.

"There you go, sweetheart." She let Clementine out of the carrier. "Aren't you pretty?"

Clementine's nails were painted peach, to match Maddie's toes. It was adorable.

Maddie tossed her coat on the chair in the hall and began unloading groceries. That morning, her stainless steel side-by-side refrigerator had contained three stalks of wilted celery, mustard, a bottle of white wine, a couple of withered onions, and a handful of carrots, purchased during a fit of culinary optimism.

Now it held food. Or at least, ingredients for food. For someone who knew how to cook. Which she was going to be. Soon.

A buzzing sound came from her purse on the hall table. Maddie considered ignoring it. Joanie was like a bloodhound on a trail, when her daughters were under stress, and Maddie wasn't ready to talk about it yet.

But it could also be Mick. He had her number, after all.

She picked up the phone. She could always let it go to voice mail. But to her surprise, the display showed an east coast number.

DeeDee.

Quickly, she hit the talk button.

"Hey," she said.

"Hey, yourself." Her twin spoke as if it hadn't been nearly two months since they'd talked in any real depth. "How's it going?"

"Good." Maddie frowned. Something was off in Dee-Dee's voice. "What's wrong?"

"Nothing! I'm great. Everything's great out here. What makes you think something's wrong? Can't I call my sister to talk?"

"Sure." Maddie glanced at the clock. It was almost five o'clock in Montana which meant eight or nine or maybe ten in New York, she could never remember the time change. "But it's Friday night. You wouldn't sacrifice prime date time for a casual check-in."

"Maybe I miss you."

"I hope you don't need a kidney. I'm saving one in case I run short of rent money."

A short, sharp bark of laughter sounded in her ear.

"You? According to Mom, you're single-handedly changing the real estate market in Montana."

Maddie went to the overstuffed armchair next to her TV and curled up with her feet tucked beneath her. Clementine immediately jumped up to join her. "And you are poised to be on the cover of *Elle* and *People* and *Cosmo* all at once."

The line went quiet. Then DeeDee said, "She may be

overstating things. Slightly."

"I guessed. Same here. Are you finally ready to come home?"

DeeDee made a rude noise. "Back to the sticks? Once you've lived in the Big Apple, sis, you're ruined for cowboys and department stores. You know who I met the other day? Ralph Lauren."

"You did not."

"Well. I met his publicist's assistant. We were in the same restaurant. Close enough. He noticed me. I'm pretty sure."

"Desperation is tough to miss."

"Love you too. How's Norm? According to Mom, he's fabulous, ready to run a marathon, leap tall buildings, cure cancer, that sort of thing. He sounded tired, to me."

There was a forlorn sound to DeeDee's voice and some-how, her concern over their stepfather touched Maddie more than she expected. DeeDee wasn't known, historically, for her selflessness.

"He's tired of Mom force-feeding him acai and spinach smoothies."

If sheer determination could make a man well, Joanie really would have Norm leaping tall buildings. Maddie had never seen such steel in her mother before.

"She loves him." DeeDee's voice was uncharacteristically soft. "Did you ever think she could be such a hard ass?"

Maddie's throat tightened. She'd missed this so much.

"DeeDee, when are you coming home?"

Instantly, a wall came up between them.

"When I'm ready."

"When will that be?"

"You have to stop asking." DeeDee took a deep breath. "What's new with you?"

She didn't want DeeDee to worry about her, on top of whatever else was bothering her. So, no talking about work.

"I tried volunteering," she said. "At the hospital. It was awful. Turns out I'm not as Florence Nightingale-y as I hoped."

Mick, in a dimly lit room, clutching her hand. Kissing her.

"You've met someone," DeeDee said suddenly.

Maddie froze. "What? No."

"You have. I can hear it in your voice."

"It's freaky when you do that, you know."

"I knew it. Tell me about him! I want to know everything. What's his name? What does he do? Is he rich? He's not a cowboy, is he? Oh, please, tell me he's not a cowboy."

Maddie pulled a knitted afghan over her legs, tucking it around Clementine's warm body. Even though she'd said much the same thing to Cynthia, she had to argue. "What's wrong with cowboys?"

"For starters, they all have names like Chip or Blunt or Flint and they call women sweetheart and are totally sexist."

"Chad's a cowboy and he's not like that."

"Cynthia got lucky. Quit changing the subject."

"His name's Mick and he's a pilot. I met him in the hospital, briefly. He's not from here and he's leaving soon, so it's not like that."

"But you want it to be."

"Nope. I'm off men, haven't you heard? Tell me about your love life, instead."

"Pfft. Too busy for any of that. Wait until I send you pictures of the boots I bought last week. You'll die, they're so gorgeous."

Maddie pulled the afghan more snugly around her as DeeDee chattered on about fashion and celebrities and parties she'd been to but by the time they said goodbye, she was shivering again.

Something was off about DeeDee. And Maddie didn't know what.

Chapter Six

MICK SAT IN the chair beside his hospital bed and stared down into a snow-covered courtyard. Thanks to an awesome health insurance plan, the hospital was in no hurry to kick him out. But he was about to start crawling the walls.

"Observation," he muttered.

Surely the doc was being overly cautious. Aside from being poked and prodded at various times throughout the day and night, he was mostly just sitting here, taking up space. What a waste of time and resources.

He should be out at Edge's place, cleaning it up, repairing the porch and the plumbing. He should be fixing that tire and whatever else was wrong with the Cessna.

"Good afternoon," a voice said from the doorway. "May I come in?"

A sunny, slightly throaty voice. Sexy as hell.

No. Not hell. Heaven.

Angel.

He turned his head, wincing as the sudden movement

sent a shaft of lightning up the back of his skull.

It was her. The face on the card Chad had given him. The realtor.

Lilacs and sunshine.

"Madeleine?"

She looked taken aback, as if she hadn't expected him to recognize her.

"Do you remember me?"

He pointed to the card on his night stand. "My friend Chad gave me your card. I'm Mick Meyer. Come on in. I guess he told you about my fishing lodge."

"Oh. Yes." She walked in, set her bags on the ground and shrugged off her coat. "Call me Maddie."

Maddie.

His mouth went dry.

She really was an angel. A long, streaky blond ponytail flowed over her shoulder, like coffee, toffee, and marshmallow cream. Dark, dancing eyes watched him above a mouth begging to be kissed.

Chocolate and caramel.

"You're looking better," she said. "We met briefly, the night of your accident. I was helping out in the ER. You don't recall us meeting?"

Did he? She seemed familiar. But the night was a muddled blur. There'd been so many voices, so many hands. So much light and sound and confusion. The disadvantage didn't sit well.

"I don't. It's probably for the best. I hear I wasn't very cooperative. I apologize if I was difficult."

"Not at all," she said, her cheeks pinkening. "I... I didn't do much. You were very sleepy and in a lot of pain."

The bag at her feet growled. No. That wasn't right. Bags didn't growl. He rubbed his wrist, rolled his shoulder. Winced.

"Sorry." He shook his head. "I'm not myself."

Maddie opened the bag and pulled out a hairy sock puppet with a very lifelike pink tongue.

"Oh, thank God," he said, and heaved a huge sigh. "I thought I was hallucinating."

"Mick, meet Clementine."

"I hit my head pretty hard. Is that a dog?"

"Yes, of course she's a dog. A Yorkshire terrier. We think. We're not entirely sure. Isn't she adorable?"

Clementine lifted her lip, showing off pointy white teeth.

"I'll admire from afar, thanks."

But Maddie's cell phone buzzed just then and she plunked the creature in his lap to take the call. The dog was light as air. The fur sticking out beneath the pink knitted doggy sweater was long and feather soft. He felt the growl rumbling right into the palm of his hand.

"Clem, behave." Maddie thumbed a quick text, then slipped the device into her other bag. "So you don't remember anything about that night?"

Pain. Panic. Soft hands. Calm voice.

Her voice.

Her hands.

"You helped me," he said, suddenly certain. "I remember that."

"Did I?" She tipped her head sideways. "How?"

The cool kiss of a spring breeze…

"I don't know. You held my hand, I think."

"I did." She smiled and he felt it down to his toes.

"You touched my head. You… you made me feel…"

The air thickened between them. She leaned forward.

"What? What did you feel, Mick?"

Safe. Treasured.

Beloved.

Pain flared in his cheek, like fire was coming out of his eye. He put his hand over it to cover it from the light.

"Mick?" She took the dog and put her back into the carrier. "Are you okay?"

He managed to nod. His head was an olive on a toothpick.

Beloved.

Ridiculous.

Maddie came close, reached out, then pulled back her hand.

Then touched his forehead.

Lightness filled him, stilled him, froze him, freed him. Released the olive. Tears flooded his eyes.

"Better?"

"Yeah," he whispered. "Don't stop. I remember this. You helped."

She perched on the mattress beside him and stroked his head while the pain ebbed. Her fingers were soft and smooth. Cool where he was hot, warm where he was cold.

Perfect.

"I'm glad," she said after a few minutes.

The pain receded to a dull ache, allowing him to think again. He squinted up at her. "Is that why you're here now? To sit with me again?"

He should be so lucky.

"No. You got my last volunteer shift that night." She withdrew her hands and glanced at the business card. "I'm actually here on Chad's suggestion."

Fatigue made him foggy again. Chad had told him about Maddie. Right. "The fishing lodge."

Maddie examined her nails. "Yes. If you need a realtor, I'd be happy to represent your business needs."

She sounded weird, stilted, like she was reading something off a paper.

"Can you sell it as is? I took January off to get it ready but that was before I ended up here. It's kind of a wreck." He sniffed. "Like me, I guess."

She met his gaze then. "That's my specialty."

He held out his hand. "Then we're perfect for each other."

Her eyes widened. She took his hand, her grip warm and

strong, her fingers soft. He didn't want to let go.

Then she stepped back, put her hands on her hips and shook her head. She surveyed him head to toe and seemed to come to a decision.

"You look like a hundred miles of bad road. They tell me you're supposed to be walking but here you sit. If we're going to sell that old lodge of yours we have a lot of work to do and we can't do it if you're stuck in here. Let's get you moving."

He'd move a mountain, if she wanted. Unfortunately, his body wasn't as cooperative. Mick slid his legs over the edge of the mattress, hiked up the sweat pants he was wearing in lieu of that god-awful hospital gown and took a few steps toward her.

"There," he said, taking her hand as she moved backwards. "How's that?"

She regarded him steadily. "Down the hall and back. Then we'll talk. Also, I have a reward for you."

"A reward. What?"

She shook her finger at him. "Uh-uh. Walk first."

As he gazed at her, the room started to spin, lazily, drunkenly, like a top ready to fall down. He gritted his teeth and focused on the tiny flecks of green in her honey-gold eyes.

Steady. Steady.

It was no use. The walls were closing in on him. The ceiling was slipping down, the ground coming up. He could either sit down, or fall down.

He grabbed her upper arm, heard her quick intake of breath but there was nothing to be done.

"On the other hand, pillow talk is great too, isn't it?" she said. She put her arm around him, pressing him closely to her side, and helped him back to the bed. "We'll walk later."

He eased onto the mattress and flopped his head gently back against the pillow. "If I had the energy," he said, "I'd be mortified."

"You already puked on my shoes," Maddie said. "This is nothing."

"I did not," he managed to say. He closed his eyes, willing the room to stop spinning. He could have done without that information.

"Dry heaves, but it's the thought that counts." She pressed her hand to his forehead, carefully avoiding the sutured cut that ran through his eyebrow.

The rotations slowed. Her fingers felt electric on his scalp, gently penetrating his skull, resetting the blown circuits inside his head, clearing and restoring energy meridians.

He moaned, then gulped.

Maddie laughed. "Feel good?"

"You have no idea."

Her laugh turned throaty. "That sound you made was a clue."

And to his shock and utter relief, Mick felt his body stir

in response to her bawdy chuckle.

Thank God. He wasn't completely broken, then.

This whole event was a frustrating glitch in his plans, but since he had to be here, he might as well enjoy the ministrations of a very nice girl that would soon be Chad's sister-in-law.

Ah. Another piece shifted into place in the haphazard way he was beginning to recognize. Maddie was Chad's fiancée's sister. Or something. Stepsister?

And at some point – yesterday? The day before? His friend had warned him that he'd developed protective notions toward his future sister-in-law and was not above hitting a man when he was down, should Mick find himself getting up to any shenanigans.

Shenanigans. He'd actually used that word. It was pathetic, what love did to a man.

Love. Lilacs.

Why was he thinking of spring blossoms in the middle of winter?

He struggled to sit up, but Maddie pushed him back. With one finger. And very smug about it, too.

"Slow down, Mick. You're not going to do anyone any good face down on the floor. Now, I have a meeting to get to. You're going to rest, then you're going to do whatever exercises they've given you, so that when I return, there's a little more of you to work with. How's that for a plan?"

She sounded like she ought to be smacking a riding crop

across her thigh. That smoky voice coming from that dewy-fresh skin made a dangerous, sweet-spicy combination and sent his pulse racing in a way that probably wasn't healthy for a man in his condition.

"Sir, yes, sir." He gave a weak salute.

"Oh, before I forget." She rummaged in her purse and came up with a small cellophane package. "You tried, so that's worth something, isn't it?"

She held out a piece of chocolate.

MADDIE STEPPED CAREFULLY over the frost-buckled slabs of the sidewalk leading to the front porch of the house that her clients, a young couple named Brad and Emily, were interested in. They should have been highly motivated, given that the wife appeared to be about twelve months pregnant.

Unfortunately, they were limited financially, and their wish list seemed to change every time she talked to them, so Maddie had spent a lot of time showing, with no results. However, it seemed they'd suddenly woken up to the reality of their situation, and as their own timing issue dovetailed nicely with hers, she felt better about assisting them in making a decision.

It wasn't self-serving. Their kid needed a home, after all.

"Be careful, please," she said, over her shoulder. "It's a bit icy here."

Mick's goal of selling quickly had seemed like the perfect

way to meet Elinor's deadline, but with him still in the hospital, wobbly and fuzzy from the concussion, it seemed wrong to push him.

Nothing wrong with giving these two a nudge, though.

Okay, maybe it was a little self-serving.

"This must be a lovely yard in the spring," Emily said, bloated and beaming.

"Take my arm, honey." Maddie pulled her gently toward the handrail. "We can't have you slipping, in your condition."

That child would squirt out of her like a greased watermelon on the fourth of July.

"Not to worry, my balance is amazing," Emily said. "I do an hour of yoga each day. That spot would be lovely for an herb garden, don't you think, darling?"

"Hm," Brad said.

Beneath the snow where Emily pointed lay a patch of gravelly dirt. The only thing that grew there was thistle.

Maddie knew, because she'd been showing this place since the summer, when the elderly owner moved into the May Bell Care Home.

Emily was usually quick to have a positive first impression. Brad was the one to convince here, and it wasn't going to be easy.

Maddie opened the front door and ushered them inside. Empty of furnishing, the place echoed. Dust bunnies rolled lazily across the scarred oak planks and the bulb in the hall light had burned out, making shadows loom in the corners.

"You could do so much here," she said, leading them briskly to the kitchen, where the windows overlooked the back yard and let in the last of the afternoon light. "If you knocked out this wall, put a half-wall here, you'd open up the kitchen and dining room to the family, creating a lovely sense of space and openness."

Emily nodded, her hand on her belly. "I can envision that. It would be a fun project."

"Show us the rest," Brad said.

"This is original brickwork," Maddie said, pointing to the fireplace mantel in the front room. "They don't make them like this anymore."

For a reason. The wood burning fireplace itself, like most of those found in houses of this age, would likely belch smoke and cost them more energy than it saved.

"It's so beautiful," Emily said, running slender fingers along the rough surface.

Brad bent down and peered into the chimney. He fiddled with the damper, and a skittering of ash and soot fell into the empty grate.

He coughed and flicked debris off his face.

"Some people choose to replace these old fireplaces with gas inserts," Maddie said, helping him to his feet. "It's a simple, cost-effective upgrade that will save you energy in the long run."

"But I love the smoky smell of a crackling wood fire,"

Emily said. "It's so much cozier than gas or electric. It feels real, old-fashioned, and evocative of a simpler time."

Maddie wanted to hug Emily. She saw the house as it had been in its glory, and as it could be again, with some tender loving care.

"Evocative of carbon monoxide poisoning, you mean," Brad said. "When was the chimney last cleaned?"

Romantic as a side of beef. "I'll find out for you. Let's move to the second floor. Isn't the curve of this bannister elegant? It's lovely hardwood beneath the paint, too. Imagine it refinished in a dark chocolate stain. A friend of mine bought a house of this vintage one street over, on Collier. She had it restored to fabulous results."

Samara had bought the place sight unseen, but Logan's restoration had exceeded her expectations. In more ways than one.

Maybe Logan would be available to do this one, too.

Maddie showed them the bedrooms, pointing out the wide sills on the windows, brushing past the tilting closet doors and threadbare carpets.

"If it was me," she said, when they came to the single full bathroom, "I'd move the walls of the smaller bedroom to enlarge this, and build an en suite bathroom for the master. You could put in a soaker tub and waterfall showers. With the lighting in here, it would be lovely."

"A jetted soaker tub," Emily said with a happy sigh.

"Yes," Brad said, "which this is not."

Emily's lips tightened. "I like it. Show us the back yard."

Maddie walked them through the snow-blanketed yard, grateful that the sorry state of the garden was concealed. It felt wrong, highlighting the advantages of this property that she knew would take a huge amount of work and mess before it was what Emily envisioned.

But she'd vowed to quit meddling. If they wanted to buy it, her job was to facilitate the deal. Her job depended on facilitating someone's deal, and soon.

When Brad called her cell later that day to inform her that they wanted to put in an offer, she should have been elated. She should have danced a jig on her desk and gone to Grey's to celebrate.

Instead, she told Brad about a different house she'd found that would be much better for them. Newer, a little bigger and with a pretty old-fashioned English garden facing south that Emily would adore.

She made plans to show it to them, knowing full well that the seller's closing date meant there was no chance of completing the deal before her deadline.

But when she set her cell phone onto her desk, Maddie felt the satisfaction of knowing she'd done the best for her clients.

Maybe, if she explained Mick's situation to Elinor, she'd extend the deadline.

It was her only hope.

Chapter Seven

O N MONDAY MORNING Maddie dressed with care, choosing a knee-length turquoise skirt, a high-necked white shell blouse, and a painted silk scarf in tropical tones. All items she'd bought specifically for her job, clothes meant to convey maturity, professionalism, experience. Responsibility.

Bought, but never worn.

"I look like a stuffed peacock," she muttered to the image in the mirror. Better than barn-swallow neutral, at least.

Cynthia or Sage would rock an outfit like this but on her, it felt all wrong, like a little girl playing dress-up.

She longed to let her curls fly free, to get out her favorite lipstick and the dangling earrings that made her want to dance. Let her collarbones show. Heck, maybe even a little cleavage. She wasn't a nun.

So why was she dressed as one?

But she pinned her hair back and sprayed it down, applied a light brush of powder foundation and waved the mascara wand over her lashes.

"Grow up, Maddie. This is your life now."

If she was lucky, that is.

Clementine looked at her and tucked her tail and whined.

"What?" Maddie said. "Do I smell desperate? If that's your attitude, I'm leaving you at home."

She walked into the office hoping she appeared more confident than she felt.

Elinor glanced up from her desk with a surprised smile.

"Madeleine. Hello. Does this mean you have good news for me?"

"Whoa," Tod said, rolling his chair backward. "Maddie Cash goes all church-lady on us."

Elinor's stare quelled him. "You look very professional, Madeleine. Shall we speak in private? Tod, haven't you got work to do?"

Maddie handed Elinor the documents she'd gotten from Mick, including a very basic letter of intent.

"He's still in the hospital," Maddie said, "but he's very motivated. I haven't been out to the place yet but I've done a title search and so far, everything appears to be in order. It would probably be better for him to fix it up first, and then sell it, but he's anxious to get it over and done with. And of course, I'm on side with that."

She hadn't explained to Mick exactly why her motivation lined up so nicely with his. No need for that.

Elinor examined the few documents with considerably

less enthusiasm than Maddie was hoping for.

"I thought you might be willing to extend my deadline, since you can see how serious I am about making this sale."

Elinor set the documents aside, lining the edges of the pages up carefully. Then she folded her hands together on the top of her desk. She sighed.

"This is recreation property."

"Yes," Maddie said.

"A very sizeable recreation property."

"Uh… I guess so." Bigger was better, wasn't it? More money, more commission?

"This will be a complicated deal, with far more moving parts than a residential sale." Elinor shook her head sadly. "It will take months to find a buyer, even if your client is able to get the property ready in short order. It could take months after that to negotiate terms."

Maddie's chest felt like it was full of lead. She'd been so hopeful that this would be what Elinor needed.

"However," Elinor continued, "you've surprised me in the past. Sometimes the stars align and things fall into place. Meanwhile, you're still looking for that young couple, right?"

Emily and Brad. "Yes," Maddie said. The stars would really have to align for that to work out.

But all she could do was keep on trying.

THE NEXT TIME Maddie visited, Mick was surprised and

delighted to discover that she'd brought him a gift of delicious, dark chocolate covered Himalayan salted caramels, the best he'd ever tasted.

He was mystified, though, that she wouldn't partake with him.

"It's for you," she said. "You need your strength if you're going to get to work on the lodge. Besides, I'm not hungry."

But the way she watched him while he ate said otherwise.

Mick pushed off the bed and accepted her help in staggering to the chair by the window. The exercise she forced him to do, humbling and unpleasant though it was, beat the boredom by a landslide. And not only was she more patient than the pitiless physical therapist, she was a heck of a lot prettier.

And, she talked to him while she massaged his stiff shoulder, which he enjoyed. There were worse ways to pass the time than friendly small talk with a pretty woman.

Though small talk with Maddie seemed oddly wrong, like a scoop of nonfat ice cream on peach pie.

"What kind of work does a bush pilot do, Mick?"

He winced as her fingers found a particularly sensitive spot.

"You know what would help my pain? Another piece of that chocolate."

"After. Answer the question."

He sighed. "Wilderness outfitter gigs. Transporting equipment and supplies for various companies. Helping out in wildfire season. Search and rescue from time to time. Ow."

"Man up. A restless soul, huh?"

She lightened the pressure slightly.

"The variety suits me. I like being on the move."

Maddie took a step back and gave him a once-over. The little dog snoozing in the plaid carrier lifted her head from her feet.

"Being stuck here must be making you crazy."

No, what made him crazy was her sexy smirk.

"I'll be up in the air in no time."

"Really?" she said. "I'm pretty sure pilots need two good arms to fly. Not to mention a working brain."

"It's working," he muttered. "Mostly."

"Let's try walking again. See if you can do two rounds without falling into the wall."

"I thought you were here to encourage me."

"I am! Not my fault you woke up on the wrong side of the bed." She waggled her eyebrows and cocked her head. "Besides, you felt better the instant you saw me at the door. Admit it."

She crossed her arms over her chest, making the soft mounded flesh plump gently above the neckline of her sweater. A nice green. Soothing. Jeans and boots completed the look. She reached behind herself and gathered her hair up, lifting it away from her neck as if she was hot.

She was.

A few tendrils floated out of the ponytail, down her neck, some light, some dark. She was so sure of herself.

And she wasn't wrong.

He exhaled, gathered his thoughts into more useful lines. "I don't feel worse."

Maddie laughed. "Put you in an alley and people will think you've fallen down a flight of stairs after a long night with a large bottle of bad whiskey."

"Ah," Mick said, a smile tugging at his lips. "Now I definitely feel better."

She pursed her lips and lifted her pert nose, frowning. Her expression cleared. "At least they cleaned you up. You don't reek anymore. Congratulations. Did they have to burn your clothes? Do you need me to run out to Walmart and buy you a new wardrobe?"

"Walmart? I'm more of a Goodwill shopper. But my clothes are fine." Actually, he was a Cabela's shopper, with a little LL Bean for fancy occasions. He gestured to the plastic bag hanging off the chair. "Ready and waiting for my exit papers."

Maddie picked up the bag, leaned over it, then recoiled. She pressed all the air out, then tied the bag shut, tightly. "Where's the rest of your stuff?"

"Back at the camp."

"So you're stuck with these?"

"Until I get back out there, yeah. At which time I'll hit the open sky, taking my stinky clothes with me."

Maddie sighed heavily, as if making a supreme sacrifice, and tossed the bag onto the floor beside her purse. The dog gave a little yip.

"You're taking my clothes?" Mick said.

"Relax, Crash, I'm going to wash them for you. Now, are you ready to try walking down the hall again or what?"

"I need outdoor air on my face, Angel. And then I believe there's the issue of my chocolate."

"You really like that stuff, huh?"

He nodded. "You're spoiling me. I'll need to stock up before I go."

"My friend Sage makes it," she said. "She's a genius. As soon as you're up to it, I'll take you to her store. It's amazing."

What was amazing was how much better he felt when she was around.

"Let's start with the hall," Maddie said with a smile. "We'll work our way up to the great outdoors."

"Sure you will. Something tells me your idea of outdoor adventure involves getting snow on your boots between the mall and the car."

She opened her mouth wide, then slammed it shut, her teeth making an audible click.

"You think I'm afraid to get dirty."

Apparently the filter between his brain and his mouth was broken. He glanced pointedly at her manicured fingertips. "Don't get your designer delicates in a twist. Different strokes for different folks."

She yanked on his good arm. "Get up. You need exercise. I need to yell at you. Clemmy, guard my stuff."

"Ow. Easy." She was even more beautiful annoyed. "That dog doesn't exactly help your case."

Maddie propelled him out the door, into the hallway. Thankfully, a handrail ran the full length. He needed it.

"You're lucky I'm such a wonderful person," she said, blowing a wisp of hair away from her face. "You should know, I hate hospitals. Fate brought us together and now you're so pathetic I can't walk away."

"Why the hell do you keep coming back if you hate hospitals so much?" It felt good to be up and around. The ground occasionally rolled and rippled beneath his feet but the walls seemed to stay where they belonged. He was making progress. He wasn't pathetic.

"My dad – stepdad – had a heart attack last year. We got him here in time and they saved his life. People were so good to us. I wanted to do something good, too. Pay it forward, you know?"

A nurse strode toward them. "Maddie, nice to see you again! But I heard you were done volunteering."

"I'm not here officially." Maddie's cheeks turned pink as she stopped to explain, smiling and touching her hand to the woman's shoulder before they moved on.

"How are you doing?" she asked. "Tired yet?"

"We've moved twenty feet," Mick said. "I'm good for at

least another twenty."

"Tough guy, huh?" She grinned. "We'll see about that."

She led him around another corner, to a sunlit room with upholstered chairs, a TV, and a couple of tables.

"What are we doing here?" asked Mick.

A counter ran along the back of the room, with cupboards and drawers beneath it. Maddie stooped to open one of the doors.

Another wave of dizziness washed over Mick, but it had nothing to do with his brain. What that woman did to a pair of blue jeans ought to be illegal.

"Ah ha!" said Maddie. She rose, brandishing a battered cardboard box.

"Scrabble?" Mick said.

"Scrabble," Maddie said. She put the box on a table and pulled out a chair for him. "Oh, you didn't think that the only exercise you needed was for your body, did you? I'm sorry. I should have been clearer."

She gestured for him to join her.

"I hate Scrabble." But Mick lowered himself into the chair. He'd learned to loathe the game one year as a kid, housebound with the flu. His mom was ruthless, with a seemingly endless vocabulary.

"Well, I love it."

She tipped the tiles out onto the laminate tabletop, making a light, clicking swoosh. Quickly she rummaged through them, shuffling and turning each one face down.

"Are you any good at it?"

She shrugged. "Better than my sister DeeDee. Not as good as my sister Cynthia. You?"

"I guess we'll see."

She was going to wax his ass and crow about it afterward. Maddie Cash did not seem like someone who'd be gracious in victory.

Unfortunately for her, he had no intention of letting that happen.

"Game on, Angel," he told her, gathering his tiles. "Let's see what you've got."

"SO, HOW DID you get into real estate?" Mick said. He rearranged the tiles on the wooden holder, watching the letters bounce and twist, wondering if this was part of the concussion, or if he'd suddenly developed a kind of girl-shy dyslexia.

Not that he was shy around Maddie.

He hadn't felt shy around girls since the seventh grade.

But he was hoping to impress her, preferably with a seven-letter word that would annihilate her.

BHVCDDA

No seven-letter word there.

Maddie placed her tiles on the board.

"Chaste," she said, marking her score on a pad of paper.

"With a double on the H, that's thirty points."

"Chased?" he said, squinting to read the letters upside down. "As in hunted?"

His head hurt.

"Chaste. As in pure. Undefiled."

He sniffed. "That's no fun. And you didn't answer my question."

She shrugged. "I had to pick something. I watch a lot of HGTV. Selling houses looked like fun."

"And is it still? Do you like your job?"

A shadow fell over her face. "I do. Mostly. I'm kind of a homebody, I guess. I like helping people find the place that's just right for them. Not too small, not too big."

"Just right. Like Goldilocks."

She smiled. "The cutthroat aspect isn't my thing, though. Tell me about this fishing lodge. Where you had Chad's stag. And crashed your plane."

"I didn't crash. I… wobbled. It belonged to my mom's brother Reg."

"He hated that name."

He frowned, startled. "Yeah. I talked about him?"

Her hand stilled. She swallowed. "I had to keep you awake. We talked about a lot of stuff. But you were pretty out of it. Most of it was garbled."

She'd seen him with his defenses down, half out of his mind with fear and pain.

What else had he told her?

"We called him Edge. He passed away a couple of months ago and it turns out he left it to us. With her in Billings and me all over the place, we don't have any need for it."

He put his pathetic offering down.

"Have," Maddie said. "Ten points. Nice."

"Don't patronize me. Do you think you can handle a deal like that or not?"

He picked up R, X and L.

"Of course I can."

She set down her letters.

"Nape?" said Mick.

"You know." Maddie pulled aside that mass of hair and touched the back of her neck.

He knew. He'd just wanted to see her touch herself.

"Six points, good job, Maddie." He grinned at her.

"My N makes that chasten." She grinned back, wider. "As in, I will chasten you for that remark. So that's six plus... twelve. Eighteen."

"Consider me chastened."

He played his turn, eleven points. Not bad, given his headache.

But this time he picked up S, A and R.

Surely he could do something with that. She was destroying him. And thoroughly enjoying it.

Maddie shuffled her tiles and examined the board.

"Tell me more about your uncle's property," she said.

"Didn't you get everything in the paperwork I gave you?"

"I want more than acreage and access and utilities. I want details. What kind of waterfront? How many buildings? What were they used for? Age? Condition?"

"Whoa," he said, putting a hand to his forehead. "Brain. Hurts. Talk. Slower."

Instantly, her face fell. She reached out and touched his hand. "I'm sorry, Mick. Are you okay?"

He laughed. "Kidding. I'm fine. I'll do better than tell you; I'll show you. Once they spring me from here, you'll get all the details you want."

"Great," she said, her eyes gleaming wickedly.

She slapped her letters down, one after another.

"Seven letter word. Destroys. Plus, I turned have into shave. So that's… forty one, plus fifty is… ninety-one. Your turn." She smiled sweetly at him. "I'm sorry, did I take your spot?"

"Nice work," he said, showing his teeth. "Aren't you supposed to take it easy on us poor walking wounded?"

She gazed across the table at him, her lush lips pursed in thought.

"You want me to take it easy on you? Something tells me that's not the way you play."

He returned her gaze, both challenging, neither backing down.

Then he put down two letters.

"Ax," he said. "Ex. Pa. Two double words. Forty points."

"Sad but desperate." She nodded. "You're still out of the running but at least it's a game now."

He nearly bit his tongue when she played her next letters, adding an S to his EX, to make STEAM.

"You just opened up the triple word score," he informed her.

She shrugged. "Worth the gamble. Show me what you've got."

Instead of using the triple word, he added a Y to SEX, spelling YEARN.

"Nice." Maddie swallowed. "Nice. Thirty points."

He'd never had a head injury before. He'd expected the nausea, the dizziness, the confusion.

He hadn't expected infatuation.

He wanted to kiss that little spot where her throat ticked and bobbed. Was she feeling it too?

Mick never did catch her lead, but he played his letters without exchanges and made a decent showing. By the time he could no longer endure the headache, they'd played the words quip, quit, quite, flew, time, riot, groan, believer— another seven letter bonus for Maddie—moon, honest, tender, go, if, zig, zag, ploy, and feel.

Maybe it was the brain injury, but Mick couldn't help think there was a message there.

"You okay?" Maddie asked, as she helped him back onto his bed.

He tried to nod but couldn't.

Shelli-Ann, the night nurse, followed them into the room. "Good to see you up, Mick. Time to check your blood pressure. How's the head?"

"He's really hurting," Maddie said.

She stroked the hair off his forehead, easing the throbbing that had hit an alarming level. It was such a relief to have her speak for him.

"It's time for his meds." Shelli-Ann tipped the pills into a little paper cup and handed them to Maddie, who held them to his lips. He took them like a child, beyond caring about dignity.

"BP's good," the nurse said, pulling the cuff off his arm. She looked at Maddie. "There's no mention of a girlfriend in your chart, Mick. I hope she's making you do your exercises."

Mick opened his mouth to correct her, but even that movement was too much.

"A friend," Maddie said. He could hear the smile in her voice. "A friend, and a girl, so sure, I guess girlfriend works. Tell me about the exercises and I'll make sure to come by tomorrow and help him start them."

Mick heard their soft footfalls move away from his bed. The meds started kicking in, easing the red pulse in his skull. His tight muscles relaxed into the bedding.

A friend. And a girl.

He could live with that.

For now.

Chapter Eight

TUESDAY MORNING BROUGHT the kind of sky Mick loved to fly into—crisp, clear, the cloud cover thin and high after the dump of snow. Bitterly cold, he guessed, but tolerable now that the wind had died down.

He stood at the window, clenching and unclenching his fists, fighting the pent-up energy from the endless hours of forced inactivity and still more "observation," especially since they insisted on observing him every hour, day or night. He was twitchy and dizzy and exhausted at the same time. And while everyone kept reminding him that irritability was a normal part of concussion, he'd like to see how they felt if every time they fell asleep, someone shone a light in their eyes, or jabbed a thermometer in their ears or wrapped a cuff on their arms.

Irritable. Try maniacal. Or homicidal.

He had to get out of here. He had to do something, anything.

When Dr. Jack Gallagher appeared for rounds, Mick duly answered the questions, then listened to Jack record the facts for the report the FAA required to determine his fitness to fly.

"Thirty-five-year-old male pilot with over ten thousand hours of flight time suffered a closed-head injury after a slip and fall of approximately six feet upon which his head impacted a snow-covered rocky surface," Jack said, speaking into his Bluetooth recorder. "The impact resulted in a loss of consciousness of approximately five minutes."

"Slip and fall," Mick muttered. "Sounds pretty stupid when I hear it out loud."

Jack ignored him.

"Anterior dislocation of the left humerus with mild to moderate axillary nerve damage apparent."

Mick shifted the shoulder. Spikes of pain bit into the joint but it was the oddly hot numbness that radiated down toward his elbow that worried him more. He must have bounced out while the plane was still moving.

God. What an idiot.

"Minor tear of the left posterior cruciate ligament," Jack continued. "Likely caused by hitting the dashboard upon impact."

Impact. This wasn't a crash. Aside from the tire, his plane was fine. So he had a few bumps and bruises.

His knee throbbed in dissent.

Whatever.

"The injury occurred in a remote area and the airman was transported out of the bush on foot, with the assistance of three friends, after which he was taken via private vehicle to a local emergency room for evaluation."

"Knock, knock," came a voice at the door. "You decent? Oh, my. That bruising just keeps getting more impressive, doesn't it?"

Maddie. Mick's spirits lifted immediately, distracting him from the annoying medical details.

"Just finishing up here," Jack said. "Come on in."

Today Maddie wore a cream and brown checked wool coat with a hood deeply trimmed with white fur. Low-heeled boots came up to her knees, drawing attention to her curvy thighs, hugged by pale-washed denim today. Her cheeks were kissed with pink, her caramel eyes sparkling, and her lips red and inviting. She carried with her the scent of snow and crisp winter air and in her hands was a large brown paper bag.

Beside the plaid carrier on her shoulder, from which the dog peered at him suspiciously, was another bag.

As promised, she'd laundered his clothes.

Wow.

"You look nice, too," Mick said. "How many foxes died making that coat?"

"Ignore the sarcasm, Maddie," Jack said, getting to his feet. "He's in more pain that he wants to admit."

"I wasn't being sarcastic," Mick said. "She does look nice. I just need to get out of here and Jack won't release me."

"I'll release you to the May Bell Care Home," Jack said. "I won't release you to a shack in the wilderness with no one to watch over you."

An old folk's home. Jack called it a convalescent home, but that didn't fool Mick. He should have told him he'd be staying with Chad or Eric. Or arranged for his mom to come get him.

The thought of being a burden on his friends or family made him want to rip the sheets off the bed, but given the choice, he'd stay in the hospital.

"If you do your exercises and your tests show improvement, I'll reconsider. Don't complain; it's the best offer you'll get."

"Exercises," Maddie said. "What kind of exercises?"

Jack gestured to a sheet of paper lying on Mick's bedside table. "It's all outlined there. He needs to regain strength and flexibility in his shoulder, he needs to use the brace so his knee can heal but, more importantly, he needs to work on fine motor skills, hand-eye coordination, proprioceptor and spatial awareness, that sort of thing."

"The man's got a head injury," Maddie said. "Smaller words, please."

"Sorry," Jack said. "I mean, you're not fully processing your body position, motion, and equilibrium."

"The dizzy spells," Maddie said.

"Yeah," Mick said, "I get it."

Floors that met his feet too soon or too late. A missed

hand rail. That sensation of falling when he was lying down.

"Our goal is to keep you moving, without allowing you to fall again and reinjure your brain before it's fully healed."

"I could get him a helmet," Maddie suggested.

Surely not. "Doc?"

"Just don't let him hit his head again." Jack handed her the paper.

Mick tried to grab it, but she held it away from him.

"Hey, what about crafts? Would that work for exercise?"

"No," Mick said. He didn't want to have a bunch of women watch while he made a fool of himself.

Jack pursed his lips. "That's an excellent idea. Things like sculpting, painting, or knitting are great for TBI recovery."

"No knitting," he said.

"What about cooking?" Maddie was on a roll now. "Say, a chocolate-making class?"

"You sound like you have something in mind," Jack said.

"You think the hospital would let Copper Mountain Chocolates in to do a therapy class?"

"I don't see why not. They used the community room to make gingerbread cookies recently. It was a huge hit."

Mick felt a million years old. But it was better than knitting, at least.

Maddie clapped. "Goody! It'll be such fun."

"Looks like you're in good hands," Jack said, giving Mick's shin a pat. "Have fun, Maddie."

Maddie said goodbye to the doctor, then set the bag on

Mick's bedside table and stroked her collar. "I'll have you know, this is faux fur, all the way. Hard to tell though, isn't it? I'm here to rescue you from yourself and sounds to me you need it. But if you're not in the mood..."

She crooked a brow, challenging him to spar with her.

"Better, now that you're here," he said. "I'll try to mind my manners. But aren't you supposed to be at work instead of rearranging other people's lives?"

"Werk-schmerk. Been there. Done that. Got bored. Now I'm here. You hungry?" She opened the bag and the most delicious aroma drifted into the air. Immediately, his stomach rumbled. "My mom made a spinach quiche this morning, brought some to town for me. I swear, moving out was way harder on her than it was on me. I've barely cooked for myself and, as you can see, I'm hardly starving. If anything, my clothes are tighter now."

"Fishing for compliments?"

"What?" Maddie blinked, then her cheeks flushed even pinker. But she recovered quickly. "Don't be silly. I know what I look like."

"Good," he said.

Maddie was perfect and beautiful and flawless. Surely she didn't need someone like him to confirm it.

"I'm no model," Maddie continued, pulling an aluminum pie plate from the bag. "That's DeeDee's cross to bear. My twin. The 'pretty one.' She's an actual model. But I know what I am."

A wave of déjà vu washed over him.

Pretty. Nice.

"I didn't mean—"

Lilacs, sunshine.

Beautiful.

"Of course you didn't." Next to the pie, she set two paper plates and two forks. "As I said, I'm no model. But I'm still gorgeous. In my own way."

He laughed out loud, surprising both. His irritability vanished and even his headache lowered a notch in intensity.

"You thought I was one of those girls constantly needing validation to prop up my delicate little ego? Does that really seem like me? Let's sit." She perched on the edge of his bed, then caught the leg of the chair with her toe and dragged it closer, kicked at it for him to sit down. She gestured to the meal. "There. It's a little crumpled from the bag, but I promise, it tastes delicious."

"I don't doubt it." Mick put his hand to his stomach. "This is the first time I've felt like eating since I've gotten here."

Except for the chocolate she brought.

A smile wreathed Maddie's face. "I'm so glad! This is actually one of the few dishes I've mastered, so if you like it, I can make it for you myself."

She handed him a plate, seemingly unaware of what she'd just implied.

Or maybe she hadn't implied anything.

He took a bite. Creamy, cheesy, with light flaky pastry and the tang of spinach. "This is amazing," he said, covering his mouth. "I could eat this for the rest of my life."

"Good!" She pressed her palms together in a quick little clap, pure childlike pleasure. Her eyes sparkled. She took a generous bite, herself, moaning at the flavor. "Mom, you're a genius."

"You'll have to thank her for me."

"You can thank her yourself. Since you're a friend of Chad's, she'll be inviting you for dinner any minute now. She likes to interrogate people under the guise of good, old country hospitality and Christian charity."

"Sounds ominous."

"She's harmless. But she's heard about you. From the guys. And Cynthia. And. Well. Me. She likes feeding people. Quit looking at me like that."

He sat back in the chair, struggling to keep a straight face.

"So. You want me to meet your parents."

More déjà vu. Stupid brain.

"Don't get carried away, Crash." She gathered their dishes, shook the crumbs into the trash, rinsed off the plastic forks, and put everything back into the paper bag. "Time for your exercises. Word is, if you can get walking upright like a non-intoxicated humanoid, they might release you."

"Yeah, to an old folks home."

"The May Bell Care Home? It's pretty nice there, actually. It might be perfect for you. But don't get your hopes up. You still look like death on toast."

"Gee, thanks. That humanoid stuff is harder than you'd think."

"A little color will make all the difference," she said, patting his cheek.

Her fingers were warm on his skin, there, then gone, and the cooling spot that remained triggered a memory. A sensation.

Sweet warmth.

Dark desperation.

The color purple.

Lilacs.

He closed his eyes, trying to capture it, make sense of it, but could not. It was like a dream.

Had he dreamed of Maddie?

She was still talking and he forced himself to pay attention.

"Since I'd prefer a guided tour of your fishing camp, as opposed to wandering alone with the wildlife, I kind of need you upright. So, here." She tossed his jacket onto his lap. "Put this on. We're going for a little fresh air. Think of it as trying out for the Olympic walking and breathing team. I'll be your coach!"

Had she known how badly his lungs ached for something other than conditioned, filtered, overheated hospital air?

"For you, Angel," he said, "I'll bring back the gold."

"That's the spirit," she said.

He only hoped he could keep up with her.

HE MADE IT as far as the front door. But instead of bringing relief, the chill outdoor air hit his sinuses with the force of a tsunami. He backed away and reached for the wall, hoping he didn't look as grey as he felt.

"What is it?" Maddie asked, letting the door swing shut again.

He closed his eyes and made a minute twitch he hoped she understood meant that he couldn't speak. She guided him to a nearby chair, helping him sit.

His knee throbbed, his shoulder ached but it was the kaleidoscope careening sharp and shiny on the inside of his eyelids that made him unable to move.

"Breathe, Mick." The words drifted warm and sweet against his ear, melting the shiny shards.

He breathed. In. Out.

He felt her fingers against his skull, probing, stroking, smoothing the ragged nerve endings.

"How about we start with something else, first?" He heard Maddie fiddling with something by his feet, and then his chair was moving. A wheelchair.

He wanted to quit, to go back to sleep until this was all over but he wasn't in any shape to object. The only way out of here was to face the pain and work through it.

The chair glided to a stop. He opened his eyes. They were back at his room, next to the window. She sat across from his chair, holding a purple pen in her hand.

"Turn your head to the left," she instructed. "Now to the right. Now straight. Good. Now from a distance."

She repeated the exercise, if he could call it that, at different speeds, from different directions. His head felt like it was welded to his body at the shoulder.

"If I hadn't started with a headache," he said, "I'd sure have one now."

"Yeah, sorry about that."

"You sound it."

"Listen, what else are we doing with our time? This is the recommended therapy, so that's what we're doing. Be grateful. You're the one anxious to get better so you can get out of here."

Was it his imagination or did Maddie sound miffed?

"Right. But Marietta's not such a bad place. Maybe I'll stick around a while."

She clicked the pen shut, then bent down to put it back into her bag.

"You and I both know that as soon as you get the all clear, you're getting in that little plane of yours and taking to the sky. Alaska, Colorado, British Columbia, wherever you end up, it won't be here. Look up."

She came up with a tiny flag with the words Styles Realty on it, held it above his head and put him through the same sequence.

This time, when he turned his head to the left, the wave of dizziness and nausea that hit would have brought him to his knees, if he hadn't already been sitting.

"Whoa!" Maddie slid to the edge of her chair. "Are you okay?"

If having an icepick in his skull was okay, then he was fantastic. He couldn't speak, couldn't move his head in response. The quiche she'd given him earlier lurched in his stomach.

He lifted his hand. Wait. He felt her get up, heard her heels clicking on the tile. A moment later, she returned with an ice pack.

"Sorry," she murmured, sliding it against his neck. The flannel cloth she wrapped it in protected his skin enough that he could tolerate it, barely. "Here. Let's see if this helps."

The room spun and swirled but the pain wasn't quite as acute. "Damn, I hate that thing."

"I know," she said. "But ice helps. You know it does."

Then her fingers were on his face.

He gasped as she ran them lightly over his skin, trailing the feathery soft touches along his jaw, over his temples, carefully massaging the bones around his eyes.

Gradually, the icy cold numbed the fiery pain.

As usual, it left him shaking with exhaustion.

"You're amazing, Maddie." He tried to catch her fingers.

Missed.

"Shh," she said, pressing his hand to his chest, where a different kind of ache was growing. Not pain like in his head. More of... an absence. An emptiness he hadn't been aware of.

This sweet woman with the magic hands was so willing to give and give, so generous with her time. He wanted to kiss her, could almost taste her lips, the warmth, the softness.

Strawberries. Chocolate.

Where was this coming from? She was helping him out because... because. The reason danced just beyond his mind.

"Why... are you helping me?"

"Shh," she repeated. "Don't talk."

She was a volunteer, right? No. She was here because of Chad. She was Chad's friend. Or sister. Or something.

No. She was a realtor. She wanted to sell Edge's place.

Or, she liked him.

If he'd met her under other circumstances, if he'd been whole and well and able-bodied, would he have had this same overwhelming response to her?

He knew the answer to that.

He'd have responded, all right. He'd have responded as far as she'd let him go. He was Mick Meyer. He didn't let women like Maddie go by without at least giving it a try.

But he'd met her at his worst, his weakest. He wasn't the carefree airman, here for a good time, not a long time.

He was here for a horrible time, and who knew how

long.

What woman wanted to hang with that?

Maddie, apparently.

The question was, why?

And the bigger question was, could he trust himself? He wasn't in his right mind, literally.

For a while, she stroked his skin without talking. He was almost asleep when he heard her voice again.

"I'm going straight over to talk to Sage about my idea."

He cleared his throat. "Don't do it on my account, Maddie."

"She asked for suggestions. This is a great one. We'll do it together. It'll be fun."

"Like a date?" Oops. He hadn't meant to say that out loud.

"Therapy," she said firmly. "And a favor for a friend. Two friends, counting you."

Friends. Was that what they were?

Fine. It wasn't a date. She didn't have to be quite so adamant.

"Chocolate therapy, huh?"

"You've tasted it. The stuff is magic."

She had a point.

Might as well try the chocolate cure.

WEDNESDAY MORNING, MADDIE waited at the counter of

the chocolate shop, trying unsuccessfully to capture all the heavenly flavors though her nose, wondering why on earth she'd resolved to give up the one thing she couldn't be without.

Portia backed through the door from the staff-only room at the back, a tray of sparkling copper-colored boxes on her arm.

"Hey, Maddie," she said with a smile.

She looked a little better, as if she'd gained a few much-needed pounds and caught up on her sleep.

"Hi, Portia." Maddie sighed and leaned her elbow on the counter. "I wish being around chocolate did to me what it does to you."

Portia blushed and tucked her head. She was adorable. "You still sticking to your plan?"

"Since everyone knows about it, I guess I have to. Why, oh why did I think it would be a good idea to declare my resolutions to the entire town?"

"It wasn't the whole town," said Portia. "It was just Grey's."

"On New Year's Eve."

And with Carol Bingley there. Maddie might as well have taken out an ad with the *Courier*.

Portia slid the glass display case shut and wiped her hands on a towel. "Wait. Resolutions... plural? What else have you given up? Isn't chocolate enough?"

Sage followed Portia into the front room.

"Maddie's also given up men," she said. "My advice? Save room for one, but make sure it's the right one. Hey, that works for chocolate too. I wonder if Krista could use that in her advertising."

Maddie snorted. "Do you know how many boxes of chocolates I've eaten my way through in search of one particular flavor?"

"Are we still talking about chocolate?" Sage laughed.

"If we want to keep the conversation G-rated, then yes."

Portia had gone quiet, as if uncomfortable talking about men in her condition. Her pregnancy was clearly visible on her thin frame, yet she still refused to talk about either the baby, or the baby's daddy.

Maddie knew Sage worried about her niece, but until the young woman opened up, there was little Sage or anyone could do. Even Portia's twin sister, Wren, had been unable to reach her.

That was the part that bothered her the most. Maddie'd always believed the twin bond was forever, but maybe she and DeeDee were drifting apart the same way Wren and Portia seemed to be. Maybe, like Wren, Maddie had to let DeeDee figure things out on her own.

Despite how DeeDee drove her crazy, it made her heart hurt to think of her going through difficulties, alone.

"Portia," she began, "I'm sorry if—"

"No, it's okay." Portia interrupted her with a raised hand. She grabbed a bottle of glass cleaner and a rag. "Sage,

I'm going to polish the front window."

Maddie looked at Sage. *"Oops,"* she mouthed.

Sage waved away her concern. "When you called, you said you had an idea to run by me?"

"Yes," Maddie said, "a class. If you're still thinking of doing one."

Sage lifted her hand like a stop sign. "Portia and Rosie deal with that. I'll be there if I have to, but they do the planning."

Maddie knew how much Sage hated promotion and marketing, but she also suspected that engaging Portia in this aspect of the business was Sage's way of making her niece feel needed.

Portia continued wiping the pristine glass. "It's for your own good, Sage. The post-Christmas slump is killing us. What do you have in mind, Maddie?"

Maddie explained how a basic chocolate-making class would appeal to certain hospital patients.

"Chocolate therapy." Portia paused, pursed her lips, then nodded. "Could work. I'll call the hospital tomorrow and set it up."

Sage frowned at Portia's lukewarm response. "It's a great idea, Maddie. You're a genius."

Maddie patted her hair. "I have my moments."

"I wonder..." Sage paused dramatically and turned her gaze to the ceiling. "Is there any chance that a certain injured pilot might be behind this scheme?"

But before Maddie could respond, the bells above the door tinkled and a gust of wintery air blew in. A man walked in slapping snow off his gloves. Nice. Young, fit, well-groomed. No one she'd ever seen before.

"Saved by the bell," Sage said, under her breath. She turned to the customer with her usual friendly smile. "Welcome to Copper Mountain Chocolates. Snowing out there again, I take it?"

The man looked past Sage, to Portia. He opened his mouth, but then his eyes dropped to her belly. His jaw sagged and his eyes grew even wider.

"Portia?" He sounded half-strangled.

The young woman stood frozen, her back pressed against the plate-glass window, staring. Her lips nearly as white as her complexion. Again, she clutched her belly but this time it was a protective gesture, as if she wanted to curl around the tiny being inside her.

The man blinked rapidly, his jaw working as if he was searching for words. Then he muttered a curse, spun on his heel, and yanked open the door.

When the icy air hit Portia, she sucked in a huge breath, gasping as if she'd been under water. She braced an arm against the nearest display case, shaking hard enough to make the glass rattle.

"Portia, honey, are you all right?" Sage rushed to her side.

Maddie ran to the door, in time to see the man leap into

a decked-out long-box black truck with elaborate pin striping along the sides. He skidded out of his parking spot, peeled out into the sparse traffic of Main Street, and disappeared.

"Who was that?" Maddie said.

"Get her some water." Sage gestured to the bottle sitting to the side of the cash register. "Here, sit down. Have a drink."

Maddie and Sage helped her to one of the chairs set aside to make room for the class.

"What's going on?" Sage squeezed Portia's shoulder gently. "Do we need a doctor?"

"No." She shook her head, wincing as if the movement hurt. "It's nothing. I'm fine."

"Bull." Sage looked frantic. "I know shock when I see it."

Maddie snatched an almond and macadamia nut cluster from the demonstration plate. "Here," she said, shoving it at Portia. "Eat this. It'll help."

Portia sniffed, a sad little laugh catching in her throat. "You and your chocolate."

"Do it," Sage agreed. "Glucose. For the baby."

Portia nibbled on the candy while Sage and Maddie exchanged glances. Who was that man?

A moment later, Portia pushed back her chair. "I'm better now. Sorry, I'll get back to work."

Her cheeks had a little color in them again, but her hand still shook.

"Forget it, girl." Sage pressed her back. "You're going

home, to bed."

"I'll be fine," Portia said. "I just need to sit down for a few minutes, okay?"

"I can call Dakota in to help."

Portia shook her head and began untying her apron, her fingers trembling on the knot at the back.

"Dakota's busy. I'm fine. I am."

Maddie untied it for her.

"Portia," she said, "what's going on? Who was that?"

Portia's gaze grew distant. She turned her face to the window, then the cash register, then the door to the back room, as if the answers she sought were hidden somewhere in the sweetness of her aunt's little store.

"No one important," she stated. "Just a guy I knew in college."

Sage and Maddie exchanged a glance.

"He's not my baby's father, if that's what you're thinking." Avoiding their questioning gazes, Portia swiped her rag over the window glass, smearing the already-clean surface.

Chapter Nine

MADDIE'S FRIEND SAGE had wasted no time, Mick thought, as he sat at the long table in the hospital community room. About a dozen patients were there, many of them in wheelchairs, most accompanied by a spouse or friend or family member.

He had Maddie.

He wasn't the only male in attendance, though he was the only one under the age of eighty. He had to admit, he was glad she'd strong-armed him into this. It wasn't just the chocolate. Being around Maddie always made him feel better.

She leaned over to whisper in his ear. "Are you superstitious? It's Friday the thirteenth."

Every pilot was a little bit superstitious. But he wasn't in the air, so what was the worst that could happen?

"Nah," he replied.

If anything, the night had good luck written all over it. Maddie was here, his head felt better than it had in days, and the aroma of melting chocolate filled the room.

And, again, Maddie was here. That trumped everything.

"Homemade chocolates are a wonderful way to treat yourself, or someone you care about," Sage said, smoothing the Copper Mountain Chocolates apron over her slim hips.

Nice, but not as nice as Maddie's curvier figure.

"With Valentine's Day just around the corner," she continued, while handing out equipment and supplies, "it's the perfect time to learn to make these chocolate covered salted caramel cups. Nothing says love like these delicious morsels, but I won't be upset if you may want to keep a few for yourself. The store's not open around the clock, after all."

This brought a chuckle from the group.

"However, our focus is on making Valentine's Day gifts, so you'll all be going home with a perfectly wrapped package to present to your special someone."

This town, it seemed, was full of people living out their happily-ever-afters, determinedly evangelizing the paired-up status to anyone currently outside the club.

Worse than ex-smokers, they were.

He noticed Sage watching them, a tiny smile at the corner of her mouth.

"For those of you who haven't met him," she said, "let me introduce Mick Meyer. He's a pilot who flew in to Marietta recently and had a little mishap thanks to the storm. He's staying with us while he mends."

Mishap. Mick felt heat prickle up his neck as various people greeted him.

He recognized Cynthia, and Shelli-Ann, the night nurse, a couple of aides and several patients he'd seen in the day room, but trying to put names to the rest of the faces worsened the twinge so he just nodded.

"This class is part of Mick's physical therapy," Maddie said, stroking him lightly across the back. "Isn't he being a good sport?"

Mick's cheeks grew even warmer, but he stood up halfway and gave a wobbly bow. They seemed a friendly bunch and what the heck, so what if he made a fool of himself in front of a bunch of strangers? If nothing else, there'd be chocolate at the end of it.

"Maddie's quite persuasive." He grinned, gesturing to her. "She's going above and beyond in her efforts to run me out of town."

Laughter rippled over the group.

"I doubt that," Cynthia said.

"The process of making candy can be tricky, even with these shortcuts, but no matter what they look like in the end, I guarantee that they'll taste delicious." Sage's gaze slid to him as if she expected his would turn out the worst.

His hand twitched. Damn it. This was not the time for the tremor to kick in.

"You okay?" Maddie whispered.

"Fine," he said. "But if I end up spilling chocolate all over you, remember, you asked for it."

Immediately, the image of Maddie, wearing nothing but

chocolate, came into his head. Suddenly it wasn't just his hand twitching.

"Yummy." Maddie's pink tongue darted out to lick her top lip, as if she had a window into his brain. Which didn't help.

Sage continued with her instructions, but Mick didn't hear any of it. He hadn't meant to flirt with Maddie.

Had he?

And was she flirting back with him?

Definitely.

Pain lanced through his temple and he pressed his fingers against it.

"Mick." Instantly, Maddie was all concern. "What is it?"

"Nothing. I'm fine."

The pain came so quickly and with such blinding white savagery, he could only grip the table top and hope he didn't pass out. Darkness shrouded the edges of his vision. The miasma of rotting garbage filled his head. His stomach flopped over inside him.

Not now, not now. Not here.

"It's okay," came a voice in his ear.

Maddie. He put all his energy into focusing on her voice, beckoning to him, like a vision in soft purples and greens at the end of a long black tunnel. Her fingers were in his hair, on his neck, pressing, massaging, pushing away the stench, killing the pain, forcing the darkness to recede.

Lilacs. Sunshine.

He kept his eyes closed, just listening to her voice, walking toward the image, letting himself fall into the rhythmic motion of her fingers. Slowly his stomach went back to where it belonged. The spasm eased and the bright, white pain faded. Awareness returned and, with it, the rich sweetness of chocolate filled his nose again.

Sage was still talking. People around him were stirring and dipping things. No one had noticed.

Gratitude rushed over him. The episode was over. He hadn't embarrassed himself.

"You okay?" she asked quietly.

He nodded, moving slowly so as not to trigger a recurrence. "Thank you."

"Would you like to leave? It's fine, if you do. I can take you back to your room. Whatever you want, Mick."

Whatever he wanted.

It was weird. He was used to dealing with women with agendas. Most of the time, especially if they met in a bar, their agendas lined up with his own, which was just fine.

When their agendas went further than that, he let them down, gently, but firmly. There was always another job calling him elsewhere anyway, so it worked.

But here he was, grounded, with a sexy, laughing, available woman who treated him like a project for her girl scout merit badge. And nothing more.

Except Edge's lodge, of course.

Which was fine. That aligned with his goals, too.

But was he imagining the spark between them? Didn't she feel it too? Or was he that broken? He tightened his lips. He simply had to get the arm working, rehab the knee, blow the fog out of his brain.

Get cleared to fly again. Get back to normal.

The sound of the side door opening made them all look up. A young woman entered the activity room. She was tying a Copper Mountain Chocolates apron loosely over her waist.

"Portia!" Sage smiled widely and beckoned the girl to join her at the teaching station. "This is my niece, who works with me at the shop. We're so lucky to have her here tonight. She's got a gift for working with chocolate."

"Hi, everyone," Portia said, fussing with her apron.

She lifted her head briefly to smile at the room but quickly turned her attention to the box of microwaveable dishes that needed distributing.

"Hey, Portia," Maddie said. She hurried over to take the box from the younger woman's hands. "You shouldn't be lifting, should you?"

Portia's cheeks flooded with color. She blinked hard and didn't look up from what she was doing. "I'm fine, Maddie. Uh, Sage, I forgot something in the truck. I'll be right back."

Sage touched her on the shoulder. "Sure, honey, take your time."

As soon as Portia left the room, Sage drew Maddie aside. Uh-oh. Someone was in trouble.

"I'm sorry, Sage," Maddie said, pressing her fist to her

upper lip. "I didn't mean to embarrass her."

"It's okay, Maddie. I know you meant well, but she doesn't want any attention. At all. Portia's pregnancy," she explained to Mick in a low voice, "is a... complicated situation. We're letting her take the lead, being supportive but not prying. It's a tough time."

"I just wanted to help." Maddie shook her head.

"What's the big deal?" Mick asked. Maddie had done nothing wrong that he could see. "That baby bump isn't invisible. What's everyone supposed to do, ignore it?"

As one, the women swung their heads in his direction.

"What?" He looked to Maddie. "What did I say?"

Mick sat back in his seat, crossing his arms in front of him. Women. They just didn't make sense to him.

Then Maddie leaned over, gently pressing her soft shoulder against his. He awaited the rush of pain that accompanied movement of the healing joint, but it didn't come. She'd found just the right angle to touch him without hurting him.

"Thanks," she whispered. Her breath was warm against his neck.

"What for?" he whispered back.

He kept still, hoping she'd stay close. The warmth of her flesh felt good against him.

She paused, then lifted her hand and lightly stroked the spot between his shoulder blades, a gesture he'd come to associate with her.

She shrugged, then smiled up at him. "Just because."

He opened his mouth to respond but before he could, Sage clapped her hands to gather everyone's attention and the moment was gone.

MADDIE WAS TOSSING a squeaky toy into the dining room for Clementine, while arranging a showing of the house she'd chosen for Brad and Emily, when she got a text from Mick.

They're setting me free today. Want to see the lodge? If you drive, I'll show you around.

Today!

She lowered her phone. He'd been improving steadily, walking now under his own steam, but surely the episode last night had not been a good sign.

She'd expected them to keep him another day or two, at least. But if Jack said Mick could go, then he must be ready.

Right?

Congratulations! She'd texted back. *Will be there ASAP.*

Brad and Emily hadn't gotten back to her yet anyway.

"*National Geographic*, or soap operas?" she asked Clementine.

The dog cocked her head, as if knowing she was being sidelined.

"Nature, it is." Maddie set up the TV.

She'd text her mom to take Clem out for a potty walk in a couple of hours, if the meeting ran late. Joanie had the idea that Clemmy might be the closest thing she'd ever get to a grandchild. Just wait until Cynthia and Chad announced their happy news!

Maddie chose a heavy parka and sturdy boots, fumbling with the laces in her excitement. The preliminary searches on Mick's property showed that everything was in order. His uncle had left his ducks neatly in a row. But she'd almost given up on this working out.

She should have had more faith.

The weather had deteriorated since yesterday, but if they hurried, she could still get some decent photos. Photos would show Elinor she was serious. Maddie was good with a camera. No matter how rough the actual buildings might be, she could get shots that would showcase the wild beauty of the setting, the openness, the sky, the mountains.

By the time she got to the hospital, she had it all worked out in her mind.

She knocked on the door leading to Mick's room.

He was sitting on the edge of the bed, fully-dressed in the clothes she'd washed, with his heavy, winter parka lying next to him. A clipboard of papers sat on his lap.

"Hey there," he said. "Thanks for coming."

"*De nada.* Guess that class was a good idea after all, huh?"

"You were right." He tipped his head toward the pages. "I'm out as soon as I finish autographing this."

The clipboard, which he held against his legs with his left

hand, was shaking. With jerky moves, he scribbled what she guessed was his signature.

"You sure you're not having a seizure?" she asked. "That's pretty bad."

He arched his eyebrow at her, then winced as the stitches moved. "Never joke about seizures to a pilot."

"Who's joking?" She lifted the papers from his hand. "You might as well have left an 'x', like the people who can't read or write."

"You're just full of sunshine today, aren't you? Where's your itty-bitty land shark?"

"Clementine? At home, safe and warm. I'll send her your love."

Jack Gallagher entered the room. "Good morning, Mick. Hey, Maddie, nice to see you again. How's Norm?"

It warmed her heart how everyone always asked about her stepdad. "He's good. Bored, I think. It's hard to tell with him."

"Your mom comes in for each appointment armed with so much research she's about ready to be a cardiac care nurse."

"Yeah, sorry," Maddie said. "Wikipedia." She pointed to the discharge papers. "Anything special I should know about? Things to watch for? Medications I should give him?"

"He's already filled his prescriptions. Make sure he takes them as directed. He's still prone to dizziness and disorientation and I'll emphasize again that it's important he does not fall and hit his head while he's still healing."

"Hello." Mick waved. "I'm right here."

Jack gave Mick a pointed look. "I've recommended he convalesce for at least a few more days. He should have someone watching over him, especially at night. But he's a grown man. And you've made an appointment to follow up for your flight clearance, right, Mick?"

"You bet, doc." Mick saluted the doctor. "I'll be fine."

"Excellent. Take care, Maddie. Mick, I'll see you soon at my office."

As soon as the door closed, Maddie turned to Mick. "Where will you be staying? With Chad and Cynthia?"

"They were kind enough to offer." Mick got to his feet, staggering slightly. "But we'll go to the camp first, right?"

He angled his shoulder under the strap of his pack, then grimaced as it slipped off, landing with a thud on the tile floor. His face went pale and he clutched his shoulder.

She was eager to get those photos, but he wasn't inspiring confidence. She took the pack away from him. Like taking candy from a baby.

"Maybe this isn't such a good idea," she said.

The camp was a good forty minutes into the foothills of Copper Mountain. Anders Run was another half-hour from there, to the south. "Right now, you're barely ready to walk to the elevator, let alone show me around a fishing lodge."

"I'm fine." He pushed past her, through the doorway, into the hall. "Sitting around is making me soft."

His gait was steadier than the previous day but he was obviously weak and in pain. He panted, short and fast. It was hard to see such a strong man struggling.

"Wait, Mick. I don't know about this."

"I'm a little winded. Too much time in bed."

He braced his hand against the wall, breathing in and out, slowly, deeply. He rotated his shoulder carefully, and the color returned to his face.

"Your poor girlfriends," she said. "I'd have guessed you for a guy with stamina."

Mick lifted his head, his eyebrows high. The tension in his face eased momentarily and he shot her a crooked grin. "Too much time off my feet. My *stamina* is just fine."

His breathing came easier now. Flirting seemed to be good for him.

"Is it your head?" she asked. "Or your shoulder?"

"Neck spasm," he said. "Neck, shoulder. It's better now. I'm good. Let's go, okay?"

Maddie heaved the pack onto her shoulder and followed him. She really wanted those photos. Chad and Cynthia were in Livingston shopping for wedding stuff all day, anyway, so someone had to be with him until they got back.

"Okay. Can't sell real estate without photos, after all."

He straightened up then and walked with her to the elevator, a little steadier now, she was glad to see.

When they entered the empty elevator car, Mick gestured to the panel.

"Main? Or Ground?"

"Ground." She reached past him and stamped it with her index finger.

Mick grinned.

"What?"

"I'd have found the button, but I do love a woman who takes charge."

Heat rushed into her cheeks. If flirting was good for his health, then she had an ethical obligation to participate. "If you want something done right, you've got to do it yourself."

"Oh, my Maddie," Mick said. He leaned back against the wall of the elevator. "That just leads to a lot of unnecessary loneliness. Sharing is caring, haven't you heard?"

My Maddie.

"If you weren't already brain injured, I'd punch you," she said.

"Nah, you wouldn't. You're too nice for that."

"You would remember that, wouldn't you? I hate being the nice one."

He cocked his head and blinked.

Uh-oh. They'd only talked about the whole nice/pretty dichotomy on what she referred to in her mind as the Night of the Kiss. She needed to distract him, quickly. She swiped at the back of her coat.

"Is there something on my butt? I feel like there's something there."

He glanced down, then up again, a little smile tickling

his lips. "Looks fine to me."

"Good, thanks. Here we go."

The door eased open. He gestured for her to walk out first and she strode ahead of him, putting her sunglasses on. She was past the sliding glass doors that led to the parking lot, outside in the biting cold before she turned around.

Mick leaned against a bench near the door, his gloves on the ground at his feet. He'd bent his head so that his hair fell over his face, but she could easily see that his skin was white, his features clenched tight.

"Mick!" She rushed back to his side. "What is it?"

"Nothing," he muttered.

His lips barely moved. His eyes were shut, his brows low, his forehead furrowed, his jaw locked.

"Sit." She grabbed his arm and pushed him down onto the bench. "Gosh, I'm an idiot. It's the cold air, isn't it?"

"I'll get used to it." His voice was faint.

He lifted his good hand up to shade his face from the sun.

"You belong in bed."

"You offering?"

"Get up. I'm getting Jack to readmit you."

"No." Mick took hold of her sleeve. "I'm okay, I promise. It's the sunlight. I need my shades, that's all."

"Where are they?"

"Who knows? In someone's truck. At the camp, maybe. I'm fine, Maddie. See?" He peeled open his good eye and gave her a sickly smile. "All better."

"Right. You are the worst liar I've ever seen."

He'd clamped his lids shut again, holding his head still, breathing through his mouth. She wanted to touch the drawn skin, ease his suffering.

This is none of your business, Maddie. This is meddling. And this is a... man.

"You're head's about to explode, isn't it?" she said.

His breathing paused, then resumed. "Yeah."

She tilted her head. It would be a long ride, but he really wanted out of the hospital. If he wasn't up to walking the property with her, she could always leave him in the car, with the window cracked. She should have brought Clementine, for company.

"I shouldn't do this," she said.

"Probably not," he conceded.

"I should send you back up and instruct them to tie you to the bed."

"Interesting proposition," he said. "But not in a hospital."

"You're impossible."

"It's been suggested."

Mick was a person in trouble. And she was someone who helped people in trouble. That wasn't meddling. That he was a person who happened to be a man wasn't her fault. And it didn't matter. The crazy imaginations she'd had that first night in the ER were gone. She was over it. It wasn't real.

"All right. But if you puke in my car, I'm dumping you on the side of the road."

"See?" he said. "I knew you were a nice girl."

There it was again.

Chapter Ten

M ICK SHIFTED HIS skull against the headrest of Maddie's passenger seat, trying to find a comfortable position. The car was cute and sporty and suited her perfectly, but even with the seat all the way back, his knees were halfway to his chin and the banged up one wasn't happy about it.

Maybe it wasn't the car's fault. Maybe he should have spent another day in the hospital. He'd been... optimistic in reporting his pain levels to Doc Gallagher.

But lying around in the hospital was a waste of time and resources. Making chocolates with Maddie last night had been fun, more fun than he'd expected. Plus, he'd been tired enough at the end of it to forego his pain meds, which had definitely influenced Jack's decision.

Though he was paying for it now. It was the damn vitals checks the nursing staff did throughout the night. Every muscle in his face fought against the white light of sun on snow that sliced through his lids, as he waited for the throbbing in his head to subside.

It was just a headache. He was fine.

Or, at least, he would be.

Peace and quiet, that was all he needed. Even before the accident, he'd been pushing hard, he knew that now. All the rush and crush at his mom's place, Edge's funeral, all the people, distant relatives he'd never met before, second cousins, great aunts and uncles, it was exhausting.

Then the shock of having Edge's old hunting lodge foisted upon him.

The weekend checking it out with the guys had been fun, for sure. But it hadn't been restful.

He hadn't slept properly since his mom's frantic phone message had called him back to Montana in the middle of the night. What a mess.

No wonder he'd stumbled and nearly cracked his cranium.

He shuddered, grateful he'd had all his faculties while he'd been in the air. Adrenaline was a great thing. He'd always had fantastic focus, when he needed it.

He hoped to hell it would return.

Maddie turned off the highway, her low-profile tires bump-bumping over hardened ruts, jostling his shoulder.

"You okay?" she asked, glancing at him.

He nodded, regretting it immediately. His skull felt like it was too small for his brain. The motion of the car wasn't doing him any favors.

"Still going in the right direction?" she asked.

"You bet."

He shouldn't have suggested she drive him. One of the guys would certainly have picked him up.

But he remembered the sensation of her fingers massaging through his hair, over his scalp, around his ears, against his temples, sending rivers of heat pouring across nerve endings, bliss riding hand in hand with agony.

Her soft voice, telling him he'd be okay.

"I'm serious," she said. "If you start yarking, you're out of here. I won't take time to slow down. This is a new car."

He smiled. "I'm okay."

"Oh yeah, I can tell. I particularly like that junkie-withdrawal thing you've got going on. The greenish-grey tint, very flattering."

She was a cautious driver. She peered both ways twice, at stop signs. She stuck to the speed limit. She avoided the worst of the bumps and potholes.

Maybe she was doing it for his sake. Maybe she was normally a terror on the road. That seemed more her style.

But what did he know? She was a stranger to him.

The vehicle slowed and Mick lifted his head.

"The Edge." Maddie read the sign at the side of the road. "Is this where we turn?"

"Yup."

She resumed but at a slower speed now that they were on gravel. Mick shifted against the seat and found a better position for his shoulder, noticing with relief that the pain had abated slightly and with it the nausea.

He wondered how her car would do on the last bit, where the gravel road narrowed. Eric had cleared the wind-sculpted drifts off the long, winding driveway, so they could get in and out for their weekend, but it had snowed a lot since then.

"The edge of what?" Maddie asked, breaking into his thoughts.

"Hm?" The lull and warmth of the drive, plus the temporary abdication of responsibility had him nearly nodding off.

"The sign."

"Oh." He straightened in his seat and adjusted the visor against the glare.

The angle was better now. No longer the high skull-splitting beam that had struck him in the hospital parking lot.

"My uncle's name is Edge. Reg – Reginald, actually, but everyone called him Edge."

She smiled. "I know."

"Am I repeating myself?"

He turned his face to the window, hating that he couldn't trust his own brain. He hated that she knew things about him, about that awful night, that he couldn't remember. But somehow he knew she would hold the knowledge with care and tenderness.

Because that was who she was.

"This is all his land?"

"Yeah." He turned to look out the window where a small herd of antelope lifted their heads to watch them pass. "I can't believe it's ours now."

"The Edge," Maddie said. "Sounds ominous. The edge of reason. The edge of darkness. They could make a movie out here. Like *Fargo*, or something."

Mick laughed. "Apparently Edge used to call it The edge of sanity."

"That doesn't sound promising."

"Common mistake. Uncle Edge once told my mom that it's the outside that's crazy. This place was where he regained his senses."

Maddie slowed more as the road tightened to a single lane.

"This is the last narrow stretch," Mick said. "Almost there."

Maddie drove down the gently curving approach and there was the cabin. It hadn't seemed so bad when it was just him and the guys, with their winter camping gear, their canned goods, and propane stove and snowbank chilled beer.

But he tried to see it from her viewpoint. The simple ranch-style cedar lodge, the panels weathered to a dull grey, a gap-toothed porch, standing drunkenly beneath a sagging roofline. The woodshed off to the side, its slant-roof rotted open to the sky, the remains of ancient split logs composting beneath it. The dock that ran to the frozen lake, snow almost but not quite concealing the missing planks.

"It needs work," he said, "but Logan assured me the bones are sound. It's not as bad as it looks."

"Definitely a fixer-upper. A handyman special."

He could tell she was not impressed. Why should she be? It would be a ton of work for her, it wouldn't show well, and with the size of it, they weren't likely to attract any offers for some time.

But if he didn't list it, there was no reason for them to see each other.

Why this thought brought such sadness, he couldn't say.

"Listen," he said, "there's no rush. In fact, if you don't want to take it on, I understand. And don't worry about getting me to Chad's. I have a few things to do here first. He can pick me up later."

He reached for the door handle.

Click. The lock flipped over.

He looked at Maddie. She shifted in her seat and crossed her arms over her chest, her eyes flashing.

"Not so fast, buddy."

MADDIE SMILED WHEN Mick jiggled the door handle.

If Mick Meyer thought she was going to leave him here in this dump, all alone, in the middle of winter, with spotty cell service and no electricity or running water, he really was nuts.

"I offered to drive you, I offered to sell your place, and I offered to drop you at Chad and Cynthia's. As soon as I've taken my photos, that's exactly what I intend to do."

"Maddie, you don't need to do that. Chad can come get me. And maybe listing now is premature. We'll have a better chance of selling in spring, once we've done the improvements."

Spring would be too late. She needed to sell it – at least list it – soon.

"I'm the professional," she said. "Leave the timing to me."

She turned off the engine and lifted the park brake, making the car rock.

Mick flinched at the movement.

"You okay?"

"Dandy." He spoke through his teeth. He'd gone grey around the lips again. "Let's do this."

Maddie bit her lip. He was barely capable of walking from the car to the cabin, let alone touring her around the property. She was going to have some stern words for Doctor Jack Gallagher when she returned to town. Letting a man in this kind of condition leave the hospital. Surely that was malpractice or something.

No, it wasn't, she remembered. People were allowed to check themselves out against medical advice if they signed a waiver.

"Did you leave against medical advice?"

He didn't answer, just let his head fall against the cool glass of the car window.

"You idiot. You're recovering from a head injury!" She took pleasure in his reflexive wince. "See? That's not even yelling, either, so don't tell me you're fine. And you want me to leave you here? Alone? What exactly do you plan to do out here if you fall down again?"

"I'm not going to fall *down*. I'm going to fall *asleep*. Something you and that medieval torture chamber called a hospital have prevented me from doing for what feels like an eternity. It's a wonder I haven't lost my mind."

Maddie released the brake, put the car in reverse and hit the gas, cranking the wheel. A dull skidding thump sounded as the wheels struggled over a drift.

"What are you doing?" Mick moaned and grabbed his head with both hands. "Maddie, please. I can't argue with you. Just let me out."

She took her foot off the gas and looked at him. Misery was etched in every line of his face. Beads of moisture glistened at his hairline. His hands were shaking.

She exhaled loudly. "You're not helping either of us, you know."

"S'not about you, Angel," he muttered.

Great. Now he was slurring his words. She changed gear, and the engine revved, but the car didn't move. She'd beached it on the drift. Great. Now she'd have to dig out before she could leave.

"What happened to no more meddling?" she asked herself as she got out of the driver's seat. She slammed the door behind her, stomped through the snow, and yanked open Mick's door.

He'd already undone his seat belt but instead of stepping out, he slid sideways in his seat.

"Whoa, buddy," she said, bracing his big body with her own.

"I'm good." He gave his head a shake, then recoiled, his face contorted in pain. But he managed to get his feet under him.

Maddie slung his arm over her shoulder – or slipped under his shoulder, was more like it – and together they hobbled to the porch.

"Watch out. Use the bridge."

Mick indicated a board lying between the step and the door, covering the jagged wood and the holes beneath.

"Sure," said Maddie. "That looks real safe."

The unlocked door opened easily. Mick stumbled inside, going straight to the long couch sitting next to a black wood-burning stove. Carefully, without taking off his jacket, he lowered himself to it, stretching out until his booted feet hung over the edge, shedding snow onto the scarred plank floor.

"Oh, that's better," he said. He lifted one arm and draped it over his face. "You, Madeleine Cash, are a true angel of mercy. Thank you for the ride. Take your pictures and go. Chad'll be here any time."

Maddie looked around the place, her spirits falling. "Mick, I can't leave you here. There's probably rats in the walls. Do you have food? Running water? Heat? Electricity?"

"Generator and candles in there," he said, waving a hand in the vague direction of the next room. "Some canned goods left. Lots of firewood."

"They're going to name me in the wrongful death suit, aren't they?"

This was what she got for getting involved in the first place. She should have walked past his room that first night, left him to suffer alone in his hospital bed. This was Dave's fault. He shouldn't have asked for her help. She wasn't a nurse, after all.

But she'd offered, hadn't she? Good-deed Maddie.

There was a fine line between good deeds and inserting herself where she didn't belong.

And now, this was where she was.

She pulled the door shut behind her, though she guessed the temperature inside wasn't much warmer than the great outdoors. She exhaled. Yup. Could still see her breath.

But the door seemed solid and she felt no drafts. There were two windows on the front wall, overlooking where she'd left her car. Neither had curtains but the inch or so of dust and bug-guts did the job.

"Ugh. You guys stayed here?"

"Nice, huh?" Mick sounded like he was half asleep.

A countertop and bank of cabinets ran the length of the center wall and she guessed this was the kitchen. "You never answered about the running water."

"Pump room's in the back. The well feeds off the lake. There's a bucket somewhere."

Maddie shook her head. Then another thought, a worse one, struck her.

"Where's the bathroom?"

Mick gave a grunt of laughter that turned into a groan of pain. "Outside."

"Right. No indoor plumbing." She slapped her arms against her sides. Things just got personal. "So, here's what's going to happen. You have your little rest. I'm going outside to see if this place has a good side to photograph. Then we're going to gather your things and drive you to Chad and Cynthia's place. It's either that or I'm delivering you back to the loving arms of our friend Dave, with instructions to hang you by a meat hook if that's what it takes to keep you there."

"Sure, sure." Mick's mumble was barely audible.

She stomped to the door and yanked it open.

"What I should do is leave you to die an ignominious death by falling into your own outhouse." She shuddered.

BUT FOR ALL his fatigue, after a minute or two – or ten, twenty at the most – Mick popped awake. No way he was letting Maddie explore this place on her own, not with the way the wind was picking up outside. She seemed like the kind of girl who would get lost in a snow squall, the one who, if an old well happened to be uncovered, would fall into it.

He slid his legs over the edge of the couch and sat up. No lightning through his skull. Good. He rolled his shoulder and stretched out his knee. Good and good.

Progress.

He stood up, waiting for the room to tilt and dip.

It stayed where it was.

Better and best. He could deal with the pain but he hated the dizzy spells, the random unpredictability. The embarrassment. The lack of control.

He zipped his jacket up to his chin, tugged his knitted toque low on his forehead and opened the front door.

The cold air bit into his sinuses, immediately jolting his headache awake and making his nose run. Beautiful, icy flames pierced his eyes as the sun dropped low over the frozen lake. The light seemed unusually bright, like it was desperate to expend all its energy before being extinguished in the coming storm. White puffs plumed in front of him, in and out. In and out.

Breathe.

He swallowed and squinted. Better. Where was Maddie?

There, heading toward the shed, where she'd have a good vantage of the lodge touched with the reddish light. She was doing well, considering the heels on her boots.

At least, she would be, if her camera bag didn't keep slipping off her shoulder.

"What are you doing?" she called. "I thought you were resting."

"I was," he said. "I'm done."

She walked away and he was pleased to note that the brightness of the sun on the snow didn't make him want to throw up anymore. He shifted position so he could watch her without the glare shining directly on him.

She stopped and stood still for a moment, her head tipped to one side. She lifted the camera, aiming it at the stand of evergreens huddled at the base of the mountain, the granite and green contrasting starkly against the untouched drifts in front.

Mick wished he had his own camera with him. Maddie's joy shone through in every line of her body, radiating from the golden halo puffing out from beneath the cherry red toque, all the way to her boots, braced pigeon-toed in the snow.

She listed sideways briefly, nearly losing her balance, before regaining it with an outcast arm. Her shout of laughter carried over the chill air, striking his chest like an arrow.

She turned, saw him watching her, and lifted her bare hand in an enthusiastic wave.

"I'm getting some great shots," she called. "It's beautiful out here."

"It is," he answered, but he doubted she'd be able to

hear.

Maddie Cash didn't care that her mascara was all worn off and that she'd have chapped lips and hat-head at the end of the day. She was enjoying herself, her spirit free and unencumbered.

He'd never met a woman like her before.

She tromped back to him, her hair trailing behind her like a golden sail.

"Got 'em," she said, breathlessly.

She staggered a bit and put her hand back to catch herself against the rough wall of the shed. The camera bag slipped again, this time clanking against her knee. She muttered a curse.

He walked quickly to close the distance between them. "Let me take that for you."

He reached for it, but his shoulder chose that moment to remind him it was still healing.

Maddie laughed. "Nice try, macho man. You need me more than I need you."

The light words hit him with an unexpected wallop and with them, came a warning.

He did need her.

He wanted her, yearned to discover everything about her, to learn if she was indeed the woman his heart, for some reason, insisted he'd been waiting for.

But she was a butterfly, beautiful, drifting from place to place, alighting for a time, only to fly off again. Needing no one.

Funny, people had always said that about him.

He tugged at the collar of his coat. It was uncomfortable being on the other end of the equation.

"Someone needs to keep you from hurting yourself."

She laughed. "You mean, like falling and hitting your head on a block of ice? Pots and kettles, my friend. Hey, turn sideways and face the lodge, yes, right there. Put your hands in your pockets. Quickly. It's freezing out here."

He heard a series of quick clicks.

"Nice," she said. "Very nice."

"Especially with the bruises. You can't use photos with people in them on your listings, can you?"

"No," she said. "But when the perfect shot presents itself, I can't resist. Here. See for yourself."

She brushed some snow off the viewing screen and held it out to him.

He walked nearer and looked over her shoulder. The fragrance of shampoo, fresh, like sunshine, or lilacs in springtime struck him in the solar plexus and he inhaled reflexively, quenching some deep thirst he didn't know he had and couldn't identify. Her breath was touched with mint, but still, it warmed the wintery air around her... her breath... and her skin and the sparks in her eyes...

"Nice, huh?" she said.

He blinked and reluctantly forced his thoughts away from mint and spring lilacs and summer. She'd captured him with his face in shadow, hiding the bruises. But still.

"It's a picture of a broken-down lodge and a broken-down guy."

She elbowed him in the arm. "No, silly. Come on, you've got a good eye, I can tell. What do you see?"

The composition was good, with the roofline and the evergreens at the front creating a strong visual frame. The golden-pink glow of the waning light warmed the building and threw interesting shadows, softening lines and edges that in full, unforgiving light appeared starkly lacking. Boring. Ugly.

Too bad the light hadn't worked that kind of magic on him.

"You've got a gift with a camera. I suppose you could always crop me out."

She shook her head, sighed. "Oh, Mick. This isn't going on any MLS site. This could be the cover of a romance novel. A strong, silent, hero, all hunched and brooding, ready to do battle to save his home from the storm. Look at that chiseled profile, those haunted eyes, that determination."

"You can see all that?"

The frank admiration in her voice made bubbles rise inside him, but he tried not to let them show.

"The image is a metaphor. You see a broken building and a broken man. I see strength. Resilience. Potential."

Potential.

"That's what my mom said, early on," Mick said.

In the first rush of grief after Edge's death, she wondered if they should fix it up and run it. In Edge's memory.

Her lawyer, her accountant, her friends, and even Mick himself had talked her out of it.

"Are you considering keeping it?" Maddie lowered the camera. "I mean, I don't want to rush you into selling."

"Mom doesn't need the hassle. This is so remote and I wouldn't be around enough to help her."

"But you could be."

"Live here? With my mom? Not my style."

Maddie cocked her head, as if considering whether or not he was telling the truth.

"Yeah," she said, finally. "Selling is better. Your uncle wanted you to have the money, to give your mom more freedom, not tie her down."

"Right," Mick said.

But Edge had already left her so much money. The proceeds of this property would hardly make a difference. She was already free.

"And of course, as half-owner, you'll make a nice chunk of change."

"Is that your professional assessment?"

She winked. "No numbers until you sign with me. But I promise I'll make you a very happy man."

She was flirting with him again and there was no doubt in his mind that she was doing it to secure the sale.

But he couldn't resist her. She was fun and she'd been so kind.

Nice.

In the back of his mind, something nudged and niggled at him, a shadowy memory, thin as mist, disappearing when he looked at it straight on. Something about Maddie. Something important.

But that was ridiculous. Wasn't it?

"I'll sign as soon as I've called my mom," he said. "Just to be sure."

"When's the last time you spoke to her?"

He thought back. "A few weeks, I guess."

Maddie turned around, shock widening her eyes. "A few weeks? You mean she doesn't know you nearly killed yourself?"

Mick winced. "No need to overdramatize it. I slipped on the ice."

"You nearly crashed your plane. You were hospitalized! Mick, you are a horrible son. What's her number? I'm calling her myself."

She reached into his jacket pocket and grabbed for his cell phone.

"It was a parking accident," he said, twisting away from her. Lame or not, that was definitely the version he'd tell his mom.

But she persisted, her grasp quick and sure.

"Ah-ha!" she said, holding the device up in triumph.

He launched himself at her but lost his footing and before he knew it, they were both down, limbs entangled, their fall broken by a thick, powdery drift.

"Hel-*lo*, cowboy." Maddie blinked up at him, her voice breathless.

Her cheeks were pink, her caramel-colored eyes dark and shining. Ice crystals laced her lashes. Her lips were inches from his, red, soft, inviting.

Mick didn't feel the snow melting against his neck, or the jolt to his shoulder and knee. Even the pain in his head and neck was background noise. All he felt was Maddie, warm and soft beneath him, her thigh between his, her knee pressed against him, her hand between them, so near his…

"Strawberry pancakes," he murmured. "Chocolate."

An elbow connected with his ribs. "What? Hey, Crash, snap out of it."

She struggled and squirmed and reality returned. She was his realtor. He was her client. Whatever weird ideas he had of them being… anything that might justify a situation like this, well. It was wrong.

Stupid!

He levered himself upright. "God, Maddie, I'm so sorry. Are you okay?"

She reached for his arm and together they stumbled to their feet.

"How's your head? How many fingers am I holding up? Mick? Can you hear me?"

The words spilled out of her and her anxiety sent a rush of unexpected warmth through him.

Mick laughed, then winced and put a hand to his temple.

"Seriously! Talk to me, Mick. Oh, my God, I've got to get you back to the hospital. Jack specifically said that you can't afford to hit your head again without possibly, I don't know, turning you into a turnip. This is horrible. I should never have driven you out here."

She started dragging him to her car. He inhaled to answer, but the cold air spasmed his lungs and he was coughing and laughing at the same time.

"What year is it?" she demanded. "Who's the president? What's your name?"

"Maddie." It was barely a croak.

"No, no." She moaned. "You're Mick. Mick Meyer! Don't you remember?"

"Honey, hold up," he said, his voice hoarse.

He bent forward, his hands braced on his knees, wheezing, unable to unlock his chest.

"Breathe, Mick. Breathe. It's going to be okay." She rubbed her hand across his back and even with the layers between them, he felt the same magic he felt from her bare hands.

"I'm fine," he said, finally. "What were you going to do, sling me over your shoulder like a cave woman?"

She stood stock still in front of him.

"Are you... laughing?" Rage quivered in her voice.

He straightened up, still chuckling. "Oh, come on. It's funny."

She lifted both hands and pushed him in the chest, hard. It hurt.

"I thought you were having a seizure. Or an aneurysm. Or a... a heart attack."

She stepped back and clutched the top of her jacket, holding it together against the wind. Her teeth chattered. She was shivering.

He stopped laughing. She was honestly and truly scared. For him.

"Hey, honey, come on. Let's get you inside. You're freezing."

"And that p-p-place will be better?"

"The wood stove will get you warmed up in no time."

In the short time they'd been outside, the sun had disappeared into the trees beyond the far edge of the lake. The wind had increased and sharp, stinging pebbles of icy snow had begun to fall.

He glanced at the driveway. They'd barely gotten through it on the way in. If they wanted to get out, they'd better do it soon.

But when they reached the porch, the dull ache in his sinuses moved to the back of his neck, and the ground had begun to ripple and tilt, reminding him his strength could disappear at any time, without a moment's notice.

Maddie pushed through the door ahead of him and shone the flashlight on his face.

He winced and held up his hand. "Quit that. Go sit down. I need to start a fire for you."

"You sit down. You're the one with brain damage. Let me feel your neck."

"Concussion. Mild. I'm fine." But he let her push him down onto the couch.

"'Just a little chest pain.' That's what my dad said. On the way to the hospital. Shove over."

She slid her fingers down into the collar of his jacket.

Instantly, he went still. A muffled groan slipped out.

"Mick, you're hard as a rock! No wonder you're in pain."

"Darlin'," he said, through clenched teeth, "do you hear yourself?"

"I mean," she said with elaborate emphasis, "that your muscles all feel like they've been welded together. I thought you had a headache. And here it's your shoulder that's been bothering you?"

She dug her fingers into the flesh of his neck until he thought the top of his head was going to pop off. Every stretched and torn fiber attaching his arm to his body screamed in protest. Tears sprang into his eyes. Speaking was utterly out of the question. Thinking was difficult. Breathing was a challenge. Every beat of his heart sent fresh heat searing along jangled nerve endings. The physical therapy he'd been doing didn't cause him this much pain. Was Maddie killing him?

Could he stop her, if she was?

Did he care?

Gradually, his vision cleared and the agony turned to something softer, a low, dull ache. Experimentally, he shifted his shoulder, rotated his head, ready for the explosion of fresh pain. It didn't come.

"Okay, things are loosening up nicely," Maddie said. She was breathing hard, harder than she had been during their hike. "Feel any better?"

He tried to speak but nothing came out. He cleared his throat, swallowed and tried again.

"Great," he croaked. Nice.

"Liar." Her fingers crept upward into his hair, putting gentle pressure over his scalp. The sensation was that of warm rain trickling down his head. It was beyond exquisite, bringing shades of soothing blue and green and violet to the edges of his vision.

"So… good…"

"Excellent." She pressed her hands onto the tops of his shoulders one last time before stepping away. "Now, I'm going to go dig my car out of the snow, and then we're going. To Anders Run or the hospital. Your choice."

Chapter Eleven

S NOW STUNG MADDIE'S cheeks. Her eyes watered. Her nose and lips were numb.

And it turned out the fold-up shovel her mother made her keep in her car – this was Montana, after all – was not there. She'd used it last fall to dig out a clump of tickseed or sneezeweed or something to plant outside Norm's window, and forgotten it there.

Improvising with an ice scraper was less effective than she'd hoped. Thank goodness she had her winter emergency kit.

She gazed out at the sky, now fully dark. The snow came down sideways in the headlight beams and the wind had picked up even more.

Where was Chad? Shouldn't he be here by now? There was no way she was getting out of here under her own steam. She slammed out of the car and stomped through the snow to Edge's lodge.

"Any luck?" Mick said. He was lying on the couch again, with one arm over his forehead.

"No. How's your head?"

"Perfection."

"Right." She pulled out her cell phone. "Um, I don't see any bars."

"Yeah," Mick said. "Cell service is iffy. Storm isn't helping."

"Great. I can't wait until Chad gets here. What's taking him so long?"

Mick said nothing, a suspicious silence that made Maddie's blood pressure go up. She walked over to him.

"Mick? He's still coming, right? You made arrangements with him, like you said, right?"

He didn't move. "About that."

"Mick!"

"I told him I'd call if I needed him."

"And he believed that?"

"He knew you'd be here."

She smacked him on the chest. "Yeah, for an hour or two."

"We'll be fine, Maddie."

"Really? Trapped in an ice-storm out here in the boonies without heat or food or cell service? What about that sounds fine to you, huh? Oh, and don't forget, you recently suffered a skull fracture, among other injuries."

"A mild concussion that's improving every day."

She paced to the window, willing herself not to cry.

She heard Mick get off the couch and come up behind

her.

"Don't touch me," she said, shaking off his arm. "This is all your fault. If you die out here, I'll never forgive you."

"Maddie, I'm sorry." His tone was soft. "I didn't mean for you to get stuck out here with me."

"No. You meant for me to leave you here to die alone."

He put his arm around her and gathered her close. His chuckle rumbled from his chest into her back, warming her.

"Nobody's dying. Chad will come by in the morning. I'm sorry you're scared, and this is probably selfish but I'm not sorry you're here with me. I'm glad you can't leave."

Oh. The glow inside her intensified. Sure, she was attracted. She'd have to be half-dead to resist him. But she pulled away. It was still freezing in the cabin and that wasn't good for him.

"Okay, you're sorry, selfish, and I'm in charge of keeping you alive. Now what?"

He gestured to the wood stove. "I'll make a fire."

He took a stumbling step toward the wood pile, winced, and put a hand to his head.

"Lie down before you fall down," she said. "I'll make the fire."

He looked awful again. She should have known better than to bring him out here in the first place. Why did she always go off half-cocked like this? When would she learn to think more carefully before she acted?

He eased himself back onto the couch. "You know how

to do that?"

She held up her kit. "I was a girl scout. I'm prepared."

He waved a hand, as if he wanted to argue but didn't have the energy.

Unfortunately, it turned out the matches were gone, given to a hot biker guy, back when she was into hot biker guys. The blanket and candle had been used on a picnic with some cowboy she barely remembered and might well have been called Chip or Blunt or Flint, as DeeDee said.

She bit back a laugh that bordered on hysteria.

No! Focus!

Her first aid kit contained two Band-Aids and a nail trimmer. The lone energy bar was hard as a brick.

But she had chocolate, in her bag.

And a book called *How to Survive in the Wilderness*.

"Any chance you've got matches?" she asked.

He pointed to a low table near the stove. "Over there. Everything you need."

"I'm all set then," she said. "A hot fire and a nice cup of tea, coming your way."

"Right."

"I can do this."

She would do this. She tugged off her gloves and blew onto her cupped hands. Building a fire was a basic human skill, wasn't it? She shook the box of matches. Half full, that was good.

The pile of old newspapers in the basket might house any

array of vermin, with the pile of split logs as backup.

She pulled the handle of the stove and it opened with a rusty screech. Ashes drifted down onto her boots from the remains of the last fire the guys had made.

It was pretty full. Did she have to take out the charred leftovers, first? She looked over at Mick. He was shivering, his face drawn tight with pain.

She should have known this would be too much for him. She should have known he was the last person who could reliably assess his condition. She should definitely have known not to back her stupid car into a stupid snowdrift.

With her stupid emergency kit pillaged to uselessness.

Well. No point bemoaning the situation. It was what it was.

She went to the area of the lodge that she imagined served as the kitchen. The cabinets were empty, but boxes on the counter contained what was left of the supplies from their trip.

A box of pop tarts. A jar of instant coffee and some tea bags. A half a bag of stale hot dog buns. A single package of instant hot chocolate mix that would make Sage weep. A couple of marshmallows. Potato chips and cheese nibs until the end of time, though. And they were set in the condiment department.

It was awfully quiet over on the couch.

"Good news," she said. "How's a toasted mustard and potato chip sandwich sound?"

"Let me sleep." Mick's voice was thick with gravel and his teeth were chattering.

She quickly pulled off her coat and spread it over him. She'd warm up soon enough once she got a fire going, but immobile as he was, he must be freezing. And hungry.

"What are you doing?" He tried to push the coat off but she held it on him.

"You're cold. And crabby. I'm the adult right now, so you have to listen to me."

"Aren't I lucky?"

She was afraid he was in far more pain than he was willing to admit. Post-concussion syndrome. She'd looked it up. Dizziness, mood swings, ripping-roaring headaches, trouble focusing.

She'd looked it up, then ignored it, so she could get him out here and get her darn photographs. Because her job was that important.

"Here," she said, waving one of Sage's chocolate nut clusters under his nose. "Eat this. It'll improve your mood."

He risked a peek. "No salted caramels?"

"You're going to be picky? Now?"

He bit into the candy. A strange expression passed over his face.

"What?"

"Mm," he said. "Déjà vu."

"Head injury," she said. "Finish it."

She tucked the cellophane bag back into her purse. He'd

need some more later.

"Aren't you having any?"

"I've had plenty," she said, pulling out the wilderness survival book and turning to the chapter titled *How to Build a Fire*.

"Step one," she read. "Using such material as bark, leaves, paper, cardboard, or other dry tinder, build your base."

She glanced over at Mick. "Any chance you've got bark, leaves, or other dry tinder hanging around?"

"Use the paper," he said. "Crumple it up into balls."

"Balls," she said. "Got it."

Given the paper supply, it didn't take long.

Step two proved more problematic.

"Layer twigs over it, then larger sticks and branches, leaving plenty of room for air. I have no twigs, sticks or branches."

"What are you doing?" Mick said, without moving.

"Making tea."

He huffed. "Sounds good. Put lots of milk and sugar in mine, will you, Angel?"

"You got it, Crash."

She closed the book. Wait. She had cardboard.

Maddie ripped the cover and back off the book, then tore them into long, thin strips. Then she yanked the first fifty pages free as well. She'd read less than a chapter, but if this worked, she'd have gotten her money's worth and then some.

"You should have some chocolate," he murmured.

"Later."

She balled up the pages, then laid the strips of cardboard on top, followed by the bark and finally, the smallest, thinnest of the split wood pieces.

"Come on, baby," she murmured, striking the first match. "Light my fire."

A draft put it out before she'd had a chance to set it to the paper.

"Is this some kind of positive thinking exercise?" Mick said. "Imagine a fire and you'll be warmer?"

"Is it working?"

How many matches were in a box? She shook the box. That sounded like a lot.

She struck the second one, guarding the tiny flame with her hand. She held it to the paper and it caught, the edge curling up as the orange fire ate into it, leaving nothing but black ash. But before it reached the nearest strip of the heavier cover stock, the flame fizzled.

"Oh, come on." Maddie gritted her teeth and pulled out another match.

She struck it but it broke before lighting up.

Her hand was shaking hard now. This had to be terrible for Mick. It felt colder than it had been a few minutes ago. Could they really survive here all night?

She blinked back hot tears, willing back the panic. She

was exaggerating, surely. Catastrophizing, as her stepsister Cynthia put it. Classic Maddie, all right. Either blissfully ignorant of the problems around her, or running around like a chicken with her head cut off.

Not anymore.

That was the old Maddie. She was someone else now. New. Improved. She was sensible now, with a job, a place of her own, even a dog. Taking responsibility.

Resisting temptation. Of all kinds.

Obviously the place was survivable. Mick had spent several days here already, with guys who knew what they were doing, but still. If the guys had done it, she could too.

She ran another match against the abrasive striking surface.

"Light. Light!" She struck it again and again. "What's the matter with you?"

Finally, it burst into flame. She held the fragile, shuddering fire to the paper, praying that it would catch this time. It had to. It just had to.

She felt wetness on her cheeks and tight heat in her throat.

"Blow on it," Mick said.

She jumped. He was standing just over her shoulder. He was looking at her with gentle curiosity. She swiped at her face and let her hair fall over her cheek.

"Got something in my eye," she said.

"Blow on it, just a little," he repeated.

Maddie bent forward and puffed softly onto the flickering infant fire. It rose up, caught on a second piece of paper.

"That's it," Mick said. He squatted down beside her, his hand was on her shoulder. "You're doing good, Maddie."

She leaned down to blow on the kindling again, not trusting her voice to answer him. The flames had reached the book cover strips now. Steam was rising from the damp wood, but some of the bark had caught. To her surprise, within a minute or two, sparks snapped and popped as the wood warmed and began to glow.

"Here," Mick said, handing her more wood from the crate. "Careful. Don't ruin your nice tower."

She braced several pieces in a tee-pee shape over the small flame, then sat back on her heels. Satisfaction warred with embarrassment.

She forced herself to meet Mick's gaze. "How do you feel?"

He was smiling. "I think I'm cured."

Pride welled up within her, and premature though it might be, she chose to enjoy it.

"Must be Sage's chocolate," she said.

WARM. SOFT. DARK. Swimming, floating.

Hands pulled at him. He didn't want to come up. He wanted to stay swimming. It was so good here, so nice.

Mick. Mick!

That was his name. Someone was calling him, from far

away. There was something familiar about that voice. He liked it. But it was attached to the clutching hands, so he pulled away.

Let me sleep. Let me keep floating. The darkness is so warm.

"Mick. Mick, wake up!"

The voice wasn't so nice now. The hand slapped his face. He opened one eye. Light stabbed straight through to his brain.

He groaned and shifted away, wanting to dive back into the comforting dark warmth, away from the grabbing, slapping hands.

Something splashed onto his face. There, the ocean, warm, salty. That's where he wanted to be.

"Mickey, please, please, wake up."

He knew that sound. He didn't like it. It made him think he'd done something wrong. With great reluctance, he allowed himself to drift up to the surface.

The hand was on his face again, but not slapping. Stroking. The other one joined it, cupping his cheeks, fingers sliding across the roughness of his jaw. A different kind of warmth slid through him. Not the darkness beckoning below him or the stabbing, piercing glare above. Something light, like... butterflies.

"Thatsss nice."

"Mick! Oh, Mick!"

Not butterflies. He hazarded a squint. The stabbing light was gone. In fact, there was no light. The fingers against his skin were cold. The moisture on his cheek icy.

Maddie.

She was crying.

"Oh, thank God, Mick. You scared the living crap out of me."

"You're crying," he said. His throat was dry.

"No kidding. I'm not sure exactly what a coma looks like but I think you were in one."

His head hurt but inside his chest, he felt good. Safe. Despite the pushing and pulling she was doing to him.

"Why are you crying?"

"Well, I'm not anymore, am I?" She grunted. "I'm trying to move a two hundred pound sack of useless. Sit up. After all the trouble I went to for this tea, you're going to drink it."

Maddie. The angel with the magic fingers. She appeared to him in his darkest places, bringing light and warmth.

The darkness called to him, smooth and seductive. It would be so easy to let go into the floating warmth, to glide, watching the pain drift far, far away, until it was gone.

But there was no Maddie in the darkness.

Maddie was here, with the light and the pain.

He lifted his hand, reached out for her, cupped the back of her neck and pulled her down. When her lips touched his, a great sigh welled up within him, like he'd just finished a marathon, or had reached the end of a long, turbulent flight. She was here and, yes, there was pain, but the closer she was, the less he felt it.

Her hands were on his face, touching him again with their exquisite, perfect knowledge, sending pleasure – yes, pleasure – across broken nerves. He breathed in her perfume, strawberries and lilacs, soft and sweet from the sun. Her hair flowed like seawater over his skin, through his fingers, tickling, settling, bringing warmth wherever it found rest.

She tasted like seawater too, wet, alive, salty. He opened his mouth, wanting all of her, more, closer. Their tongues danced together, warm, wet, familiar and foreign at the same time.

Was he imagining this? Had he slipped into another magical dream? This wasn't the dark place, but perhaps the darkness wanted him so badly it could conjure up the very thing, the one thing, that could seduce him without question.

He didn't even know this woman, yet he felt like she was a part of him.

"Maddie," he whispered.

She pulled her mouth from his and rested her forehead against his cheek.

"What was that?" she asked.

"Are you real?"

"What?"

"Is this…" He struggled to find the right word. "This… kissing. Is it real? I can't tell."

Maddie sat up. Cold air rushed into the places where

they'd been together and he tried to bring her back. The dark floating warmth was nothing compared to the sensation of her lips on his. He needed it more than anything in his life.

"Who knows, Mick? I'm the last one to ask. Can you sit up now?"

The crying sound was back in her voice. He liked the dark but now he wanted to be able to see her, see if he could figure out why she was sad when a moment ago, she'd tasted so... happy.

"You're the only one to ask, Maddie. If you don't know... who does?"

"All I know," Maddie said, "is that it always feels real. Until it doesn't."

He heard pain in her words, as if her heart was bleeding and the blood had turned airborne, rising, shimmering from her throat to his ears, where they pierced like shards of ice and left him aching.

"You're shivering," she said. "I'll put some more wood in the stove."

She stood up. Too far away. He struggled to a sitting position and pain knifed through his skull, slicing emotion to one side, bringing thought to the forefront.

Strangely, he preferred the emotion.

Without thought or logic or sex or any of the usual parameters that guided his so-called love life, his heart felt right.

After attending to the fire, Maddie sat down beside him again. The cushion dipped and rolled as she shifted them until his head lay in her lap. So soft. So warm.

"How's this?" she said.

"Perfect. Best date ever."

"A date. You're hilarious. This is a life-and-death situation. It's about as far away from a date as humanly possible."

She sounded so adamant. It was cute. He was going to enjoy changing her mind.

"Technically," he said, "we're spending the night together. I think calling it a date would be okay, under the circumstances."

Part of him wished they could stay in Edge's awful cabin forever.

She nudged him with her knee. "I should have left you to the mercies of the elements."

"I could have made a fire."

She snorted. "You'd be bear food by now, if not for me."

"Hm," he said, snuggling deeper into her softness. "Maybe. Got any chocolate covered caramels in that goody bag of yours?"

"Of course," Maddie said.

"And you'll eat some, too?"

He didn't know why it bugged him that she refused to eat any, when she so obviously wanted it.

"We'll see," she said.

"Yeah," he said, "we will."

As the cool blue light of dawn broke through the dark night, Mick imagined putting a piece of luscious chocolate onto Maddie's tongue, watching her eyes roll shut, listening to her moan with pleasure. He was going to get her to admit her hunger.

He wasn't leaving Marietta until he did.

MADDIE ADDED MORE wood to the embers burning in the stove. Turned out there had been a nice dry cache on the porch that Mick had forgotten about. She'd almost cried when she'd found it.

The only thing worse than being stranded at the edge of sanity was being stranded there at four in the morning.

Mick's episode had left her too shaken to sleep. She curled up on the other end of the couch, with his feet in her lap, and tucked the comforter up higher around them both.

Then she nudged him.

"Hey, time for proof of life. You breathing?"

Mick inhaled and exhaled audibly. "Happy?"

He didn't appreciate being awakened and she didn't blame him, but she wasn't about to take another chance.

"Ecstatic."

A spark popped inside the stove. The wind had died down, but snow continued to fall outside, blanketing the world with stillness and calm. It was actually peaceful.

Romantic, even.

Aside from Mick trying to die on her.

"You mentioned you had a twin sister," Mick said. His voice was faint, his words slow.

"What?" She was too tired to talk. She tucked her head down onto her arm. She'd just rest her eyes for a minute.

"Fraternal, not identical, you said."

"DeeDee," she mumbled. "She's the pretty one."

Mick snorted. "If you say so."

"Wait until you see her."

"I've seen you. Don't need to see her."

He tossed the words at her casually and they landed soft and warm in a place she hadn't even known was cold.

"That's nice of you." But she wasn't playing games anymore. She was being honest. Even when it hurt.

"DeeDee's a true beauty," she admitted now. "She's a half-inch taller than me. Her cheekbones are higher. Her lips fuller, her legs longer, her hips narrower. She's just..." She hesitated, searching for the right word. "More."

I miss my sister.

The thought caught Maddie by surprise. She was angry that DeeDee had deserted the family, but now she realized that she was hurt, too. She felt about her twin the same way she felt about her left arm. It was part of her. Always there, but not something she thought about. Until it was gone.

Mick looked her up and down. "Different, maybe. Not better."

Something about the way he said it made her want to

challenge him, to force him to convince her.

"Oh, yeah? You know me that well, huh?" She pressed her fist against her lips to stop them from trembling.

"I know enough," he said simply, and then closed his eyes. "Somewhere between too little and too much, that's where perfect lives. That's you, Maddie."

Chapter Twelve

A WEEK HAD passed since that disastrous, wonderful, terrifying night. A profusely apologetic Chad had rescued them in the morning, and taken responsibility for Mick, agreeing with Maddie that he couldn't stay at the lodge alone.

Logan Stafford had set his crew of wayward teens to cleaning up the lodge and was of the opinion that the work required was mostly cosmetic and could be done in a month.

She'd even had a nibble of interest from a corporate buyer hoping to steal the place with a low-ball preemptive bid. Of course, she'd advised Mick against it, and he'd agreed.

Brad and Emily were still waffling, though she couldn't blame them entirely, as they'd once more been ready to offer on the latest place she'd shown them, until she pointed out that one of Brad's deal-breakers was an attached garage, something this house lacked.

Thin icy fingers of panic tickled her stomach. She was going to lose her job because of her big mouth.

She dropped her head into her hands, grateful she was

working from her desk at home, instead of having to do this with a smile on her face, pretending everything was hunky-dory.

Her cell phone vibrated.

"Madeleine Cash," she said, without checking the display screen, hoping she sounded more professional than she felt.

She felt like a worn out dishrag. And she felt like crying.

"So, you are alive," her mother said.

Crying? Make that howling.

"Hey, Mom."

"So, now that you're a bigwig in the business world, you're too busy for your father. Is that it?"

Maddie's heart fell. Cribbage night with Norm.

"Ah, shoot. Mom, I'm so sorry." She looked at the clock on her phone. If she left right now, she could still make it to the ranch, get in a game, maybe watch a bit of TV with him. "It's been a crazy day here. I meant to text you. Tell him I'm on my way."

She felt bad about the tiny deception, but she couldn't bear the thought of her parents anticipating the evening plans that had slipped her mind entirely. She got up and started putting on her jacket.

"He's already gone to bed, Maddie."

Something in the tone of Joanie's voice made Maddie stop. "It's not even eight o'clock. Is he okay?"

"No, Madeleine, he's not." Joanie didn't bother hiding her frustration now. "He was counting on seeing you tonight and then not only did you forget, but you didn't even let him know. He went to bed with a headache. He's been snappy all day. I made your favorite chicken pot pie for supper," she added with a sigh. "I'll put it in the refrigerator."

As if Maddie needed another serving of guilt. Cynthia was over there nearly every day. Wasn't that enough?

Maddie realized it wasn't just frustration she was hearing in her mother's voice. It was fatigue. And fear.

Maybe it wasn't her stepdad that needed her.

Maybe it was her mother.

"I'm really sorry, Mom. I'll grab Clementine and we'll be there in a half hour."

She hopped into the car and pulled onto the road leading out of town toward the sprawling ranch that had been in the Henley family for generations. Fence posts whipped past her in the dark, her headlights illuminating them momentarily, bright, then dark against the snow-covered fields. Guilt gnawed at her. Norman was still in the first year after his heart attack and Joanie was doing her best but Maddie knew how hard this must be on her.

The worry. The responsibility. All alone, with a husband who'd never be very good at articulating his needs.

Mick wasn't like that. He was pigheaded, like all men, but he said what he wanted. What he needed.

He'd told her that he wanted her. That he needed her. That she was enough. Perfect.

The frisson of excitement raced down her spine again at the memory of the same dark intensity with which he'd spoken that first night.

He wasn't a man to say things like that lightly.

He wasn't a light man. He was heavy. Solid. Serious.

"Serious as a heart attack." A terrified laugh caught in her throat.

Mick really did need to have his head examined, if he thought that he could feel something real, something so... serious... for someone like her.

In such a short period of time.

It was crazy!

It didn't make sense.

And Maddie really, really didn't know what to do with it.

When she got to the ranch and entered the dimly-lit kitchen, she found her mother sitting at the table, her head in her hands.

"Mom?"

Joanie lifted her head and smiled tiredly. Tears sparkled on her cheeks. "Maddie. I didn't mean to make you feel bad, honey. You shouldn't have come. I know how busy you are."

Maddie gathered her little mother into her arms. "It's just work. How's Norm?"

"Sleeping." Joanie straightened up, ran a hand down Maddie's face. "Did I sound that pathetic on the phone?"

"Do you really have to ask?" Maddie smiled to soften her

words. "Guilt trips are your specialty, Mom. What kind of daughter would I be if I didn't play along?"

"Oh, well, in that case." Joanie sniffed, then fluffed out her hair. "I hope you haven't eaten. I might have slaved all day on that pot pie."

"In fact, I'm starving." Maddie could see the package on the counter, indicating that Joanie had cooked a store-bought pie, instead of one made from scratch, for supper that night.

"I'm sorry you made the trip all the way out here for nothing." Joanie took the pie from the oven, cut a slice and set it on a plate.

She added a serving of spinach salad, poured a glass of milk and set the meal in front of Maddie. Aside from Maddie's slice, the pie was untouched.

"Mom," she said, "haven't you eaten?"

Joanie waved a hand. "Not hungry. I suppose I forgot." She busied herself wiping the sparkling clean counter.

"Then sit down and eat with me. I hate eating alone."

Joanie blinked in surprise, as if the thought hadn't occurred to her. "Oh. All right."

Maddie watched her mother dish out another serving and sit down at the table.

"You've lost weight."

"Nothing I couldn't afford to lose."

"Okay," Maddie said, "but don't lose any more. You're scaring me, Mom."

"I'm fine." Joanie toyed with a forkful of chicken, pushing gravy in a circle, then scraping it together again. Her eyes were ringed with fatigue, grey with worry, vague and distant.

"Of course you are." Worry sharpened her voice into sarcasm. She thought of Mick's courage in admitting his fear. How could she help her mom and dad if they refused to tell her what they needed? "Will you, for once, quit being a hero? Your husband nearly died. Will you just admit to yourself that you're terrified? That your life has changed and you don't know what to do with that? How to be? Who you are anymore?"

Joanie dropped her fork. She pushed back her plate and got to her feet, knocking the chair back so that it wobbled on its legs. "You think I'm a hero? You think I don't know terror? This isn't the first time for me, Maddie. I can't lose another husband. I don't know how to do this again. I can't bear it. I can't bear... this."

Joanie walked to the sink, turned on the garbage disposal. She took her plate and scraped the entire uneaten meal into the trash, as if sleepwalking.

Maddie got up, walked up to her mom, and put her arms around her. All her own troubles disappeared as she felt the trembling, raw fear in the one woman who'd always been her rock.

"Mom." Her throat closed. "What can I do?"

"Oh, honey." Joanie shook her head slightly, as if suddenly hearing herself. "I'm so sorry. I didn't mean to unload that on you. I shouldn't have done that. I'm just tired. You're busy with your own life, all the exciting new changes you're going through. It's just as it should be. And I have no right to put my burdens on you."

"Who else?" Maddie said. "I'm your daughter. If I'm too busy for my family, then I'm too busy. Period."

The simple statement struck her with the force of a two-by-four.

That was how people coped. They set their priorities, and they worked around them.

She'd been working so hard to build herself a life, that she was missing out on that life.

And, just maybe, Mick was part of that.

MORE DAYS WENT by in a blur. As he'd told her, Mick had all the necessary documents for Edge's property. But there were still numerous other steps required before she could list it for sale. Title searches. Surveyors. Inspections.

She felt like she spent half her day on the phone, and the other half waiting in the cold, for someone to show up.

On Friday afternoon she stood beside the once ram-shackle, fishing lodge, tapping her foot. "Where is he?"

Her phone vibrated and she grabbed for it, yanking off her glove with her teeth.

It was a text, from Sage.

Wait until you see what we've got planned for tonight. You'll give up giving up chocolate immediately.

Darn. She'd forgotten about the class. She bit her lip. She hovered over the response screen, then decided against it. The inspector was due any moment. As long as he came on time, she'd make it.

Even if he wasn't on time and Maddie couldn't get there, she'd warned Sage this could happen.

"Relax," Mick said, stepping down carefully from the half-refinished porch. "He'll be here."

Behind him came the sounds of hammers and saws as Logan's crew worked their magic on the interior. She suspected the sound wasn't doing him any favors, but he was working hard to hide the pain, and she'd seen how tightly he'd gripped the porch rail.

"Says you. I'm freezing my butt off."

"Looks intact, to me. Hey! You can't hit me. I'm in-jured."

The grin on his face made her smile. Maybe he wasn't faking it. The bruising around his eye was healing, now a lovely greenish-yellow instead of purple, and he was using his arm fairly well again.

"I've got a surprise for you."

"Oh yeah?" Her spirits lifted. She loved surprises.

The sound of a vehicle drifted over the icy landscape, and she looked toward the road.

"It'll have to wait," she said, waving at the truck with relief. "The inspector's finally here."

"That's not him," he said, taking her arm. He had a mysterious smile on his face. "It's my mom."

"Your mom?"

He wanted to introduce her to his mom?

Marry me.

She shook her head. She was being silly. Mick had been out of his mind during that conversation. None of it meant anything. Her imagination was running away with itself.

"You're the one that told me to call her," Mick said, taking her arm. "Mom being Mom, she had to come make sure I was in one piece. Don't worry, you'll love her. And she'll love you."

Why would she worry about that? Why did Mick have that funny look in his eye?

The truck pulled to a halt and a woman in skinny jeans and big, fur-topped boots jumped out. When she saw her son, she stopped and put her hand to her mouth. Maddie realized that the fading bruises she'd gotten used to must be horrifying to someone who wasn't expecting them.

Mick ran to meet her halfway and threw his arms around her. Maddie recognized his reassuring tone, though she couldn't make out his words. The hug he gave her lifted the slender woman off her feet, and she gave a laughing scream of protest.

Watching the easy affection between mother and son made Maddie smile. Chad was right about Mick. He was a good guy.

"Mom, I'd like you to meet Madeleine Cash," he said,

leading his mom toward the lodge. "Maddie, this is Charlene Meyer. My mom."

"You're the one who's been taking care of him?" Charlene reached both hands toward Maddie.

Mick had her eyes, dark blue-grey, with laugh lines at the corners. Hers sparkled with tears.

"I haven't done much," Maddie said. "Oh!"

Charlene pulled her into a tight hug. "Thank you, Madeleine. Thank you."

She stood back and held Maddie at arm's length. "You're just as pretty as Mick said you were. And you must be tough, if you got someone as stubborn as him to follow doctor's orders. I'm grateful."

Maddie's cheeks heated up at the praise. Mick had been telling his mom about her?

Footsteps sounded on the porch as Logan stepped out of the building.

Mick set about making introductions and soon they were inside, admiring the work the boys had completed so far. Maddie tried to see the lodge as Charlene would. The building had improved greatly in a short time. With the battered furniture gone and the scent of fresh sawdust and paint, the place had a definite air of possibility.

Logan set a piece of plywood onto a pair of sawhorses and opened some drawings. "I have a few suggestions," he said.

Mick and Charlene bent over to study them, just as

Maddie heard the crunch of tires on snow. Finally!

She went outside to join the man with the clipboard, leading him around the property as he made notes. By the time they got to the lodge itself, the sun was long down and Logan's noisy young assistants had left. Mick showed the man around the inside, answering questions, while Maddie waited with Charlene.

"I'm sorry about your brother," Maddie said.

Again, Charlene's eyes welled up. "Thank you. It was a terrible shock. Do you have siblings?"

Maddie nodded. "Two sisters, one twin, one step."

"Cherish them," Charlene said. "I should have tried harder with Edge. I shouldn't have let him drift away."

The way DeeDee was drifting away from the family?

Maddie's phone buzzed. She recognized the name on the display a split second before she remembered the truffle class.

Sage.

"Everything okay, Maddie?" She spoke lightly but Maddie heard the undercurrent of stress. "I was wondering if you got stranded again."

"I'm so sorry, Sage!" She glanced at the time. "If I leave right now, maybe I'll make it."

"Don't bother, we finished early. Only five people showed up. I don't know what happened."

Maddie's heart sank. She knew what happened. She was supposed to remind the volunteer coordinator that another class was scheduled.

She'd forgotten.

"I'm so sorry," she repeated. "Next week will be better."

"I don't know if it's worth the effort," Sage said. "Anyway, I'm glad you're okay. Talk soon."

She hung up and Maddie was left staring at the blank screen, feeling awful, thinking back to the conversation with her mother. Bad realtor, bad sister, bad daughter, and now bad friend.

What was left?

Chapter Thirteen

MICK SAT IN the exam room at the medical center across from Marietta Hospital, waiting for Dr. Jack Gallagher to finish tapping his notes into the computer. The man was a one-finger typist and it seemed to take forever. Weren't there people to take dictation? Surely he didn't work like this every day.

"You're looking better than expected," Dr. Jack Gallagher said, finally. "Your range of motion in the shoulder is excellent. Keep doing your exercises. How are the headaches?"

Mick shrugged. "Not as bad as they were."

"You sleeping?"

"Sometimes. Not great."

"How's your memory?"

"Fine." Mostly.

"Any dizziness?"

"Only when I get up too fast."

"Any trouble with focus? Concentration?"

"No. Come on, doc, don't keep me in suspense. Are you

going to clear me or not?"

Jack tapped a pen on his desk. Mick felt exposed. He hated being in the hot seat. He wasn't a good patient and he couldn't wait until he was done with this whole business.

"Aeromedical concerns," Jack said, "are directed at the neurological sequelae that may persist for days or weeks following the acute event, sequelae such as post-concussion syndrome, focal neurological deficit, neuropsychological deficiency, and post-traumatic epilepsy."

The words washed over Mick like level five white water, bouncing him from rock to rock, knocking him breathless, afraid for his life.

Most of them were meaningless to him, but epilepsy, everyone understood that.

A diagnosis of epilepsy meant he'd never fly again.

"Focal neurological deficits cover a broad range of impairments," Jack continued, "which may include cranial nerve palsies, aphasia – the inability to speak – or hemiparesis, one sided paralysis. Most focal deficit recovery occurs within a six-month period, but full recovery may take up to three years."

Paralysis. Palsy. Inability to speak. The headache Mick denied grew, thudding hot and heavy inside his skull.

"Three years." He didn't recognize his own voice.

"Worst case scenario, Mick." Jack put his hands out in a settle-down motion. "You haven't exhibited any signs of focal deficits at this point and given your improvements, and what we've seen on your tests, I don't expect any. Our baseline neuropsych evaluation appeared normal for a man of your age. This is good news, Mick."

Mick sat back in his chair and dropped his head in his hands. "Can't wait to hear the bad."

"Traumatic brain injury is classified as mild, moderate, or severe. Mild TBI includes loss of consciousness and/or post-traumatic amnesia of less than one hour. You lost consciousness for a few minutes, and you have some memory loss, so we have to class you as mild TBI. You haven't had any seizures and that's a very good sign. But even for mild TBI, the seizure risk remains elevated for ten years after the injury."

"Ten years. From one hit on the head."

"Concussion is nothing to mess around with. The problem with pilots is that the seizure threshold is already lowered by the nature of the job. Sleep deprivation. Changes in altitude and air pressure, leading to hypoxia."

"Just tell me. Can you clear me, or not?"

"You want this to be simple, Mick. But it's not."

It was just his life.

"Nonspecific complaints such as headache, dizziness, insomnia, and irritability," Jack said, with mild emphasis on the last word, "are all typical of post-concussion syndrome. I'm surprised you aren't experiencing any memory impairment or concentration difficulties."

"I'm not."

He had to try a little harder, maybe. But surely that was to be expected.

"These symptoms are self-limiting, usually resolving within three to six months."

"So this headache could last another five months?"

Jack tipped his head. "It could."

Mick lifted his head. "Am I done, as a pilot?"

Jack pushed a piece of paper across the desk. "Mild TBI with no seizures, six months. Remain free from symptoms during this period and you'll be reinstated to flight duties. Six months, Mick, and you'll be flying again. Five months, actually, since it's already been four weeks since the accident."

Mick scanned the page from the *Guide for Aviation Medical Examiners* listing the federal regulations. So many words, such small print. But Jack had highlighted the sections he'd just spoken about.

"I'll fly again," he said.

He hadn't realized until just now exactly how terrified he'd been that it was over.

"Stay healthy and, yeah, I'd say you will. Congratulations, Mick. This is good news."

Mick left the office in a daze. He'd walk over to Bramble House where his mom was staying, to let her know the good news about his condition. Then he had to call his contact in Alaska, tell him to find someone else for the charter runs. He wouldn't be happy, but these things happened.

He pulled out his phone as he walked, but the number he brought up was Maddie's. She was the one he wanted to share his news with first. She was the one who'd cared for him, who seemed to understand, better than anyone else, how much his freedom and independence meant to him.

In telling her his good news, he'd also be telling her that he'd be around for another five months, the longest time he'd spent in one place for a lot of years. He realized he wasn't upset about it.

He was thrilled his chances of flying again were good, but he was just as happy to be sticking around. Now that he knew his old life would be there for him to pick up where he left off, he found the urgency to leave was gone. He had options. And in the meantime, Marietta wasn't such a bad place to be. Chad and Eric were here; he'd made some new friends, too.

He had the lodge to work on and the project had come to have a certain appeal for him.

Like Maddie had said, the place had potential.

Actually, she'd said something about him having potential, too.

Even though she'd seen him at his worst—cranky, painful, frightened, and angry.

What had she said? Not a broken man. Power. Potential.

A whiff of lilacs drifted over him. He glanced around. The houses were all laced in snow and frost, the trees bare. There was nothing remotely in bloom. Where did that trace of lilacs come from?

Maddie's initial enthusiasm about selling the property had eased up. After meeting Charlene, she seemed to think it might be better to give his mom more time to be sure about selling Edge's land. Perhaps she was right. There was no reason to rush into anything.

What if he took his time, fixed it up, maybe spent a little time fishing, relaxing? The guys had always told him he worked too hard, spent too much time away. Maybe they *should* consider Charlene's offhanded suggestion of reviving the business, as a kind of homage to the lost brother she'd always hoped would find his way back to the family.

How would Maddie feel about him staying in Marietta?

MADDIE HAD GONE into the office after hours, in hopes of gathering her things without an audience. The chances of her finding something for Brad and Emily grew more remote by the minute. And she'd seen the look on Charlene's face. She wasn't ready to sell Edge's place yet. Maybe she never would be.

Maddie couldn't pressure them. She wouldn't pressure them.

Charlene would keep the land, Maddie would lose her job, and Mick would fly off into the blue yonder, as he'd always planned.

Whatever Maddie thought might be happening between

the two of them wasn't real. It never had been.

Chad had warned her right at the beginning. Mick wasn't a guy who stuck around.

And she wasn't an "attaching" kind of girl.

Except it seemed she'd gotten attached to Mick.

She could seek all she wanted. But it wasn't until she gave up that she found what she'd been searching for.

She sighed and went into the staff room to get her various mugs. A delighted Clementine trotted along behind her, playing hide-and-seek in the shadows, pouncing on dust bunnies. At least she was having fun.

The clock on the wall ticked the seconds away in the silent room. Maddie kept her coat on against the chill as she emptied her desk. She'd call Brad and Emily in the morning and let them know she was handing their file over to Elinor.

Then she'd call Elinor.

The bell jingled at the top of the door and Maddie jumped. Clementine let out a startled yap.

"Who's there?"

She'd forgotten to flip the lock shut. She grabbed a butter knife from the drawer and peered around the corner to see who was arriving at the office after closing.

"Maddie? Is that you? I saw your car."

Her pulse kicked up a notch. Mick.

He saw the utensil and held up both his hands. "Put down the weapon and call off your dog, ma'am. I mean you no harm."

"You scared me." Clementine, having gotten over her initial distrust, bounced up to him and began gnawing on his boot laces.

"I left you a message." He glanced around the dimly lit room. "What are you doing here anyway?"

"Oh, you know." She gestured vaguely. "Paperwork. I don't know how things pile up. I like to work when it's quiet. No one's here to bother me. You look excited. Why do you look excited?"

She swallowed and took a breath, willing herself to stop babbling.

Mick grinned. "I just came from Jack's office."

Of course, the physical for his pilot's license.

"I take it you got good news." She was happy for him, she was. This was what he'd been waiting for. It was what he wanted. He was a pilot, he needed to fly. He'd come to Marietta for a weekend and ended up staying a month, and not by choice.

Her cheeks felt like they were frozen, her lips pulled too wide over her teeth.

Mick came close and tugged her into an embrace, then reached up and stroked the back of her head.

"Hm," he said. "You smell so good."

He smelled good, himself. He felt good, looked good, and tasted good, too. But that didn't matter.

"Dandruff shampoo," she said, pushing herself away.

She gestured to the chair, then scooted around the desk

to claim her own seat. Distance, that was what she needed. Distance and heavy furniture.

"So, when do you leave?"

"Summer." He grinned.

"Summer? That's months away." She was confused. He must be disappointed by the news, yet he seemed happy.

"Or later. Depends."

"I'm sorry, Mick. I know how you were counting on getting your license back. Are you… okay?"

If Jack hadn't cleared him, that must mean they found something bad on his tests.

He shrugged. "Recovering perfectly on track. Six months seizure free is standard after a mild concussion. I should have expected it."

"But everything else…?"

"Everything else is getting better. Slowly but surely."

Six months. It didn't make sense.

"It gives us time to finish the lodge properly. You don't mind, do you? If we don't sell right away? Sorry about the commission but I'd like to take my time."

Panic simmered. Maddie got to her feet, paced over to the copy machine.

Elinor predicted this. She'd be done with Maddie and rightly so. Tod would crow I-told-you-so and she'd have to move back in with her parents. But what did they expect? She was Maddie Cash.

She took a deep breath and rotated her shoulders. Calm,

soothing thoughts.

"It's your decision," she said faintly. "I want you to make the right one."

He strode over to her and took her hands in his. "I thought that the only thing I wanted was to get my license back and take off into the sky. Resume my life, as I've always known it."

She nodded, her throat tight. Of course that was what he wanted. It wasn't his fault she'd stupidly managed to fall in love with him.

"But you know the first thing I thought when Jack told me that I couldn't fly for at least another five months?"

She looked into his eyes and shook her head. He was gazing at her like he wanted to kiss her. That was a bad idea.

"I thought," he said, lowering his head, "that gives me five more months with you. And that I've waited far too long to do this."

She ducked out from under his arm. "Says the man with a brain injury. Marietta's not your kind of town."

"My head's fine. Maybe I've changed. Maybe I want to stay now. Take time to fix the place properly. Get to know you, also properly, without hospitals, or physical therapy or business dealings between us. Just you and me."

With every word, he'd gotten closer and now he had her back up against a filing cabinet. Somehow, she couldn't make her legs move away from him. And if her legs weren't moving, well, the rest wasn't likely to go anywhere.

You and me.

She liked the way that sounded.

"No, no, no!" Again, she scooted beneath his arm. Self-control all over the place. "I don't do this anymore. No more casual dating, no more hookups, no more… whatever this is." Maddie steeled herself to continue. "And I'm certainly not going to let you make a decision like this based on some… fantasy you've got about… us."

"What if this is more than a casual hookup?"

"Since we haven't slept together, it's not even that."

"Actually, we have," he corrected. "But I agree. It's not a hookup. And there's definitely nothing casual about us." He touched her chin, trailed one finger down her jawline. "I've watched you sleep, Maddie. I touched your hair. You held my head when I was sick and when I thought the pain was going to split me apart, you kept me together. That's not casual, honey. From the moment you swaggered into my room with that little dog on your arm, I knew. It felt as if we'd met before. Like we already knew each other. Tell me you didn't feel it, too."

No, no. It was worse than she thought. She'd tried so hard to not be her usual flirty self with him. To be business-like and professional and boring. She was done playing with men like so many toys. She'd sworn to do it, to become more than the party girl that no one took seriously.

Talk about backfire. He seriously thought he was in love with her. Which was impossible because, a—no one had ever done that before and b—

"You have a head injury, for Pete's sake! How can I trust anything you say? You shouldn't be making decisions at all right now."

"Good point," Mick said. "I'm not in my right mind, so I have to stay here and I have to stay near you because when I'm with you, I don't feel... broken."

Oh, he knew just what to say.

"Now," he said. "Let's go out and enjoy this beautiful winter night. I've gotten used to walking with you. I miss it. Show me around this pretty little town of yours. Please?"

How could she say no? Maddie collected the box containing the contents of her desk, gathered her coat, and tucked Clementine into her carrier.

"I've got Clem."

"Bring her. The fresh air will be good for her."

"Let me put this stuff in my car, okay?" she said.

He frowned. "Do you always take so much stuff home with you?"

"Oh," she said. "Realtors. We never know what we'll need."

She was going to miss the job. But this wasn't the time to think about it. Mick was happy and he wanted to be with her and she'd never told him about what had happened that first night because it hadn't been real. Nobody knew anything about that, so this was okay, she wasn't breaking any ethical boundary or dumb resolution or anything.

Just a girl, going for a walk on a Friday night in Marietta, with a handsome guy beside her.

The sky was blacker than black, but stars were out in abundance. She knew how much Mick loved the outdoors and she had to admit, the crunch of snow beneath her boots and the rush of cold air in her lungs made her understand why.

Mick grabbed her gloved hand in his. She pulled away.

He laughed. "Come on, Maddie. Take my arm. You don't want me to fall down again, do you? Think of it as a safety issue."

The whole scene was too romantic. And he'd begged her to show him around town. On foot, he'd insisted, as they would miss too much by car.

Mick pointed to the Grey's Saloon sign at the end of the block. "We should go in."

Maddie hadn't been to Grey's since making her little New Year's Eve proclamation. Walking in on the arm of a handsome man like Mick was hardly the way she intended to do it. She'd eaten enough crow in her lifetime to know she really hated it.

"You can't have alcohol yet."

"I don't need alcohol, Maddie." He stopped and faced her. "I want music. I want laughter. I want to be with a beautiful girl in a crowded bar."

Oh, how was a woman to withstand such charm? His lake-dark eyes caught the soft glow from the street lamp above them, made them blaze and sparkle, sending heat deep into her belly. All of that sounded pretty darn perfect to her.

"I've heard that Grey's on a Friday night is the place to be in Marietta," he continued. "Dancing might be an excellent way of assessing my balance and focus."

A little dancing, a little fun, perhaps a drink or two, might be just the thing to take her mind off the failures she'd had to deal with lately.

She smiled and pushed him away. "Might be a great way to break your head again, too."

He tucked one foot behind the other and twirled, putting his hands out in a ta-da gesture, marred only by a slight wobble.

"Oops. See? You've fixed me, Maddie."

Maddie swallowed.

She cleared her throat and started walking in the direction of Grey's, tipping her head in an invitation for him to follow.

Summer. He was staying until summer.

Maybe Chad was wrong. Maybe Mick was a staying kind of guy. Maybe he'd only been waiting to find the right place.

Or the right person.

Birds fluttered in her chest again.

It was the weirdest relationship she'd ever had with a man, the timeline all jumbled, backward and forward. Chaotic.

First, there was that long horrible night after his injury,

when he'd joked about them being perfect for each other, about marrying her. The kiss he begged her for, that she'd given, that was gone from his memory but remained stamped indelibly on hers.

He'd slept in her arms when they'd been stranded at Edge's place. Although there'd been nothing sexual about it, the intensity of those hours had stripped Mick naked, emotionally. Her too. She felt, believed, they'd connected on a level of intimacy far beyond physical.

She'd seen him, the real man, the tenderness beneath the rough exterior. She'd felt his beating heart, tasted his tears.

As Mick's health improved, those layers had closed up, little by little, buried by the day-to-day stuff of living. Humans were fragile creatures, needing a lot of covering to survive. They could no more live with their hearts bared than they could make it through a Montana winter night in shorts and flip-flops.

But when she and Mick looked at each other, as they talked, and got to know each other, Maddie couldn't help but believe some tiny bit of that deeper connection remained.

Is this real? He'd asked.

Could it be real?

What if it was?

They'd started out all wrong. She'd crept into his hospital bed in her usual impulsive way, with the best of intentions. Now she'd lost her heart to a guy who probably didn't even remember the hours that had so vividly changed her life.

And now, like any two normal, single adults, acquaintances responding in the usual way to a superficial attraction, they were going to have their first date.

Trust Maddie to get it all backwards.

Chapter Fourteen

MICK OPENED THE door of Grey's Saloon for Maddie. Instantly, warmth enveloped him. He stomped the snow off his boots and followed her to the bar.

The rustic ambiance was welcoming and comforting. Blake Shelton crooned about lost love in the background, on the dance floor a few girls bounced and tossed their hair, laughing and chattering, while cowboys sat at the bar and observed through hooded eyes.

"You." The barkeep gave Maddie the once-over. "Wondered how long you'd last."

"Missed you too, Jason."

Mick smiled. Small-town banter.

"Who's your date?"

To Mick's surprise, she flushed.

"We're not dating. He's actually Chad's buddy, Mick Meyer. I'm… showing him around town."

Chad's buddy?

Was that all he was to her?

"Jason Grey. This is my place." The man wiped the

counter, barely looking at them. "You keep her in line, hear?"

"Jason," Maddie protested. "It was New Year's Eve."

"You puked on my bar." Jason set down the cloth, finally noticing Mick. "Geez, pal. I hope the other guy looks worse. What'll you have?"

"Serve the lady first, *pal*," Mick said.

He didn't like the way Jason was talking to her.

Jason pulled a glass from under the counter, added a scoop of ice and several wedges of fresh-cut citrus. "The usual?" he said, without looking at Maddie.

"Iced tea, please," Maddie said, as if his comments hadn't bothered her in the least. "Sweet, with three slices of lemon."

"Long Island?" he offered.

"Virgin."

The bartender gave a bark of laughter. "Sticking to your guns, huh? We'll see."

Mick ordered a soda and lime and they carried their drinks away from the bar.

"What was that all about?"

"Nothing."

"Maddie!" A group of women waved at her. "We're having chocolate martinis," a buxom blonde called. "Join us."

"Very funny." Maddie's smile looked like it hurt. "Another time."

The group dissolved into laughter, and their circle closed, leaving her clearly on the outside.

"Friends of yours?" Mick asked. "Do you want to sit with them?"

"Nope. Inside joke. Never mind."

Maddie clutched Clementine's bag close to her chest and held herself tall, like a warrior, her shoulders back, head high.

"Hey, Maddie." A tall man dressed more business-casual than the rest of the patrons, leaned against the bar, grinning lazily at Maddie. "You just don't give up, do you?"

Like the women Maddie had walked away from, the guy seemed to be mocking her.

"Shut up, Tod." She tightened her grip on Mick's arm.

Scared? Not Maddie. So what was it?

Mick bent down to speak into Maddie's ear. "You know, for someone who's supposedly introducing *Chad's buddy* around tonight, you're doing a lousy job."

"He's nobody. But come this way. You'll like these guys." She walked toward a table of laughing denim and t-shirt clad men. As they came abreast, one of them reached out and touched her arm.

"Hey, Maddie. How's your dad doing?"

A genuine smile broke over her face, this time. "He's doing good, thanks. Mick, this is Flynn Benson. Flynn, this is Mick Meyer. He's a friend of my future brother-in-law. Mick flew in from Alaska for Chad's stag."

"Heard about that," Flynn said, putting out his hand. "Weather tipped you sideways. Good to meet you."

"Flynn runs the local search and rescue, Mick."

"Your buddies saved us a call out. How're you doing?"

Mick smiled wryly and touched his forehead. "Better. They won't let me fly yet, but I don't mind. Turns out I kind of like hanging around Marietta."

Flynn looked between him and Maddie and raised his eyebrows.

"I was in the ER the night he came in." Maddie explained quickly, her words running together. "He's stuck here while he recovers, so I've been helping out, driving him around and stuff. Chad's so busy and I've got time because… well. Hey guys! Have you met Mick?"

She clamped her lips shut as twin flags of color rose high and hectic on her cheeks.

"Let me introduce you to the Zabrinskis," Flynn said. "Also known as the Big Sky Mavericks."

A couple of men joined them from the bar, carrying drinks in each hand. Maddie relaxed visibly. More introductions were made.

Maddie's friend Sage, the chocolate maker, arrived, and the two exchanged a hug and a few quiet words. Portia, the pregnant girl, was behind her, holding a large, fruit-garnished beverage. Soon Mick had been introduced to what seemed like dozens of other friends, wives, girlfriends. It was a happy jumble of names and faces he doubted he'd be able to recall even without a concussion.

"I'm so glad to see Maddie having a good time again," Sage said, leaning confidentially to Mick. "She's been pretty bummed about her job."

Had he missed something? "What's wrong with her job?"

"Oh." Sage glanced guiltily over at Maddie. "Nothing. I meant... you know. Work... is hard. And her being so serious about everything these days. And sticking to her resolutions like she is."

"What resolutions?" This wasn't memory loss; he'd been kept out of the loop. Deliberately.

"Where has the time gone?" Sage grabbed her purse. "I've got to go. See you!"

Portia slid onto the chair in her place. Across the table, Maddie was introducing Clementine to an older gentleman in a western shirt.

"She meant Maddie's New Year's resolution to give up chocolate," Portia said. "I wasn't here to witness it firsthand but apparently she got up on the bar and made kind of a scene."

Mick glanced back at the women who'd toasted her with their martinis. It hadn't been a friendly gesture. They were still watching her with keen, predatory eyes.

"Why?"

Portia shrugged. "I'm sure it was a joke. I mean, no one believed her."

He thought of how longingly she'd looked at the chocolate caramel cups during Sage's class. And how firm she'd been in resisting. If those women were waiting for Maddie to fail, they didn't know her very well.

"After all," Portia continued, "she swore off meddling and men, too and here she is, with you."

MADDIE HAD SWORN off men? Was that why she was holding back?

But before Mick could ask her about it, the guy she'd walked away from earlier grabbed the chair next to him.

"Tod Styles." He stuck out his hand. "You're Mick Meyers. I heard Maddie's been cultivating you. I work with her. Worked, I guess I should say."

Tod's handshake was chilly and damp. Mick looked for Maddie but she was now deep in conversation with a pretty brunette that he guessed by her features to be a Zabrinski.

"It's okay." Tod leaned closer and lowered his voice. "I know she's been playing it cool. It's no secret that she lacks that killer instinct." He paused. "My condolences on your loss, by the way. You and your uncle must have been close. Here's my card. For when you get serious about selling."

Greed flashed over the man's face and he'd had too much to drink to hide it.

Mick flicked the card onto the floor. "When I decide to get serious, I have Maddie."

Tod's eyes shuttered.

He tipped his beer up, swallowed and wiped his mouth with his hand. "Right. You have Maddie."

The way he said it put Mick's back up.

"She's been very professional. Very helpful." Mick's jaw hurt. Tod clearly had an agenda.

"That's Maddie. Helping herself into unemployment. She could have sold your land three times over, as is, made you both rich."

"Sure, or wait until spring and get a better price. Wait. Unemployment?"

"She needed that sale, man. Didn't she tell you?" Tod chuckled. "When did you meet her? In the hospital? You think that was a coincidence? She knew you had land to sell. Why else would she be hanging around? The goodness of her heart? She's getting cut from the team, my friend. Her time's up. You were her best chance, probably her only chance, and she blew it."

Mick stared at him, thinking of all the time Maddie had spent with him in the past few weeks and the box she'd taken from the office and put into the trunk of her car.

Oh no. Surely she hadn't jeopardized her job by helping him with his recovery. Even if she had, it was hardly the place for a coworker to tell a client about it. This wasn't professional behavior. It was professional assassination.

He wanted to punch the smile off Tod's doughy face.

"What did she ever do to you?" Mick asked.

Tod chuckled again, bitterly this time. "She's a tease, Mick Meyer. Better you learn it now, rather than later. She's a flirt and a taker and a talker but don't count on any follow-through. She's the kind of girl who lets you hang around long enough to buy her birthday gifts and take her out for Valentine's Day and then starts counting the minutes until she drops you. You know who she was kissing on New Year's Eve this year? Me. And then minutes later, she announced to the whole town that she was swearing off men. Like I didn't even exist."

Maddie kissed this guy?

"Tod!" Maddie squeezed between them, her face white. "What are you doing?"

Tod held his palm out in a placating motion. "Hey, we're just talking. You didn't introduce us earlier so I had to do it myself."

"Leave it alone." Maddie glared daggers at the man. "Mick, let's go."

She grabbed his sleeve and hiked Clementine's carrier onto her shoulder.

"Does Jason know you brought the rat into his establishment?" Tod called after her.

"Knock it off, Tod," Sage said.

Tod was getting unfriendly looks thrown at him from more than a few faces.

"What the hell, Maddie?" Mick said, as she dragged him toward the door. "Who is that guy to you?"

"Nobody. It's nothing. I work... used to work with him. Come on. I'll drive you back to Chad's place."

She held her head high but there was a telltale tremble in her voice.

As soon as they got outside the bar, he pulled her to a stop and forced her to face him.

"Tell me what's going on. Did you lose your job because of me?"

Someone would be deeply regretful, come morning, if that were the case. He wouldn't let that stand.

"No. Of course not." She blinked and ducked deeper into her hood. "I lost my job all by myself."

Bullshit. But she seemed to believe it. She seemed to believe the worst about herself. He wouldn't let that stand anymore, either.

"What happened?"

She turned to look down the street. Her profile was backlit by the street lights and with the snow falling gently beyond the awning. A winter angel.

Angel.

Lilacs. Sunshine.

She laughed, a hiccupping sound that was half-sob.

"I decided to become a better person."

"By giving up chocolate," he said. "And men."

"Don't forget meddling." She groaned. "I thought you were the one person in Marietta who hadn't heard about that."

He thought of her fingers on his skin, the way she'd known when he was in pain, the way she made him laugh. Her enthusiasm for selling the lodge, then her encouragement about the restoration. She'd put him first, without giving him an inkling of the cost to herself.

He took a step closer, pushing her against the building. He hadn't kissed her since... since the day they'd fallen into the snow together... and the long night afterward. She'd held back, trying to maintain a certain distance. To stick to her resolution.

He leaned in.

Her eyes were huge. Her breath came in quick, short gasps.

"Don't, Mick," she whispered, as his lips neared hers.

"What's the matter, Angel?" He brushed his nose against her cheek. He could almost taste her.

Lilacs. Strawberries. Chocolate.

A rush of white agony streaked through his eye. His knee buckled and he half-collapsed against her.

"Mick!" she cried, holding him up. "Mick, what's wrong?"

He tried to tell her he was fine, that nothing was wrong, but his mouth was dry as cotton and it took him several tries to get the words out.

"Just a spasm," he managed, finally. "I'm okay."

She led him to a bench on the sidewalk and helped him sit. "You're not okay. But my car is just down the block. Are you okay to stay for a second?" She put the dog carrier beside him. "Clementine, guard Mick. I'll be right back. Then I'm taking you to the emergency room."

"Not going to happen," he said, but she was already

gone.

An uncomfortable notion quivered in the pit of his stomach. The pain was easing, but the memory that sparked it was as clear as ever.

Maddie, leaning over him in a dark room, the scent of spring lilacs swirling around her.

Maddie, stroking his head with the touch of an angel.

Maddie, kissing him with lips that tasted of chocolate and caramel and strawberries.

It wasn't his imagination. It was real.

Chapter Fifteen

MICK CONVINCED MADDIE that he wasn't dying, but not by much. She'd compromised by bringing him back to her apartment where at least, in her words, they were within spitting distance of medical assistance when his head exploded.

His head wasn't exploding. In fact, now that he'd begun to remember that first, lost night, he felt better than he had since it had happened. He wasn't losing his mind. He wasn't imagining the chemistry between him and Maddie. And with every detail that emerged through his murky memory – her firm touch on his forehead, her fingers wiping away his blood, her eyes anchoring him to the world – he craved more.

He wanted to know everything about that night.

He wanted to know everything about Maddie – not the work-Maddie or the helpful-Maddie but the Maddie-at-home.

The real Maddie.

What better place than her apartment?

"Where's Clementine?" he asked, looking around him.

Her place was tidy and decorated with homey touches. Knitted throws on the couch, tons of photos of family and friends, and furniture that he recognized from Chad's workshop.

"Sleeping. You should sit down."

"I feel great, Maddie. But I wouldn't say no to a piece of that dark chocolate caramel with the salty bits. You know," he paused. "The kind you fed me in the hospital."

She froze. "You remember that?"

The real Maddie seemed nervous.

"I remember you kissed me. That was real, right?"

She winced. "I'm sorry, I shouldn't have done that. But you were begging and, well, kind of irresistible."

"Talk to me, Maddie. About those resolutions. About your job. About that night. About… us."

"Those stupid resolutions. This has been the toughest month of my life. Do you have any idea how much I love chocolate? I'm pretty fond of meddling too."

He smiled. "And men?"

"You heard Tod." She busied herself in the kitchen. "I've had a lot of fun with a lot of guys, with no thought to their feelings. I'm selfish and impulsive and I don't think things through and I forget to look after the people who are important to me." She reached into the cupboard above her head and pulled down a box of tea bags. "I've been a spoiled brat my whole life. Immature. Irresponsible. Giving up chocolate is a small penance to become a better person."

He'd heard her on the phone with her mom. He'd seen her taking Clementine around the hospital, making people smile. She'd bent over backwards not just to help him recover, but to prevent him from making hasty decisions.

"Maddie. You might be the least selfish person I've ever met."

"It's the principle." She sniffed. "I'm a grown woman who's never succeeded at a single thing in her life. I need to prove I can do it."

"For how long? And what about men? Are you planning to join a convent, too?" Slowly, Mick rotated his left shoulder. Then he lifted his hand, opening and closing his fist. "You see this? That's because of you."

Maddie shook her head, her eyes glistening. "Your physical therapist did that."

"And who made sure I did my exercises? Who bullied me and encouraged me when I got lazy? Who massaged my head when I thought my brain was leaking out my ears? Who dragged me into a damn candy-making class because she knew it would help me?"

She looked away. "That's nothing."

"It's everything." Mick stepped directly in front of her and touched her chin. "Maddie, I couldn't have done this without you. Doesn't my opinion count? I think you're amazing. A month ago, I couldn't wait to leave. Now, I'm not sure another five months will be enough. I'm not sure I can live without you."

Maddie started and somewhere deep inside him, a bell went off.

"What?" he said. "What am I missing?"

She tucked away a small smile. "Nothing. Just… you said something similar that first night."

"Yeah," he said, reaching back into his mind. "But there was more. What else did I say?"

She swallowed. "It was silly stuff. You were rambling. In so much pain."

"What else?"

Whatever it was, he knew it was big. Her cheeks were pink.

She blinked quickly. "We were joking around. About how much we had in common, perfect strangers both wishing we were somewhere else. Talking about travel and rent and life. I thought you were living paycheck to paycheck, like me. You said… you said you couldn't live without me." She spoke softly, as if sharing a cherished memory. "Then you said… you asked me to… marry you. You were kidding, of course. I know that. But it was very sweet, all the same."

Marriage.

It came back to him in a rush, how unmoored he'd been that night, tossed in a sea of confusion and pain and how Maddie had been a life-preserver he'd grabbed onto and clung to until his feet touched bottom again.

Mick Meyer had been on his own forever, traveling all over the world, always on the move, always seeking what was over the next horizon. He lived out of his truck, or his plane, a backpack at the ready, his cell phone always on.

For the first time in his adult life, he'd been forced to stay put. He'd been dependent, unable to trust his body or even his brain, half mad with fear, desperate and lost. And then Maddie had taken his hand and led him into the light. She'd shown him it was okay to need help, that it didn't make him any less of a man.

And he finally understood why a man might want roots, as well as wings. That maybe he too could have what his friends had.

"You found me that day in the hospital and you took me on, like a stray dog," Mick said.

She touched his cheek. "I've always liked dogs."

He took courage from her shaky smile. "I've never met anyone like you, Maddie. I've certainly never proposed, joking or not. You've seen me at my worst, curled up in a ball, puking my guts out, angry, scared, alone and you didn't back away. How about you give me a chance to show you my best?"

"If I'd been the girl I was six months ago," Maddie whispered, "we'd have definitely been a thing, you and me. You were the perfect guy, after all."

"Strapped to a gurney and bleeding?"

"No," she said. "Temporary."

MEMORIES OF THE night they met washed over Maddie, in a wave so big and hard it took away her breath. She'd been frightened, but the big, macho guy punching out the ER staff had been terrified.

He didn't look terrified now. His jaw was tight, his eyes hard. But she had to stay firm.

"You're leaving, Mick," she said, her heart breaking. "Whether it's now or next summer, you're going to fly away because that's your life. Anything we think we feel for each other right now won't change that."

"You're scared," he said, flatly. "You don't trust yourself. You don't trust me."

"Would you?" She hesitated. "You're not… yourself, yet, Mick.

He was quiet.

"I've known a lot of damaged guys, Mick. Cowboys in town for the rodeo, looking for a good time, winners wanting to celebrate, losers hoping for some sympathy."

She paused, patting away the dampness on her cheek. "I've never wanted to fix them. I just wanted to have a good time, until they moved on. It worked. For me and DeeDee both, it worked. Then Cynthia was gone, all nested up with Chad and I was happy for her, I really was. I am. She deserves it." She hesitated. "I haven't always been as supportive of my stepsister as I should have been."

"If you say so." He picked up a lock of her hair and

twisted it gently around his index finger, then brought it to his lips. "That's not the Maddie I know. But go on."

It was hard to think with him so close beside her – and when had they moved to the couch, anyway? His aftershave was redolent with something woodsy and green.

"Stop distracting me." She tugged her hair away and smoothed it along the side of her neck. She had to tell him the truth about herself.

"Then, my dad had a heart attack and then DeeDee left and, you know, it turned out I didn't have as many friends as I thought." She and DeeDee had made a game of making other women jealous. It had worked. All too well.

She forced herself to continue. "I've been... careless... my whole life. Then my boss put me on probation, gave me until the end of January to make a sale, or I'd lose my job. I was so lonely on New Year's Eve that I ended up with Tod Styles. My boss's son. Who I loathe, I might add." She took a deep breath. "And then there was you."

She'd given up dating, only to stumble across the one man she truly wanted.

Mick smoothed her cheek with his thumb. "Best thing I ever did was fall out of that plane."

"I'm addicted to self-destructive behavior, Mick."

"And you think if you break your resolutions now, you'll end up staggering out of Grey's next year with a whole new list of regrets?"

"I won't let you believe I'm someone I'm not. And I

won't pretend you're someone else, either. I knew from the beginning that you weren't here to stay." Her voice trembled. "You're a month into healing from a head injury. You could be a completely different guy another month from now."

The words landed between them like live grenades.

"You really believe that, don't you?" Mick said.

Then he got to his feet, put on his jacket, and left her apartment.

Maddie pressed both palms against her face. Maybe he'd change. Maybe he'd stay the same. Regardless, she loved him. And that was why she had to let him go.

Chapter Sixteen

MICK STRODE THROUGH the doors of Styles Realty first thing the next morning.

"Elinor Styles," he demanded of the girl at the reception desk.

"Good morning, sir," she answered, unfazed. "Do you have an appointment?"

A well-dressed older woman looked up from the small counter where a coffee pot sizzled and dripped.

"Never mind." He strode past the girl. "You must be Ms. Styles. May I have a word?"

The woman was unruffled by his tone of voice. She held out a steady hand. "Elinor Styles. And you are?"

"Mick Meyer. I may have a large piece of property to sell."

"I've heard rumors. You've come to the right place, Mr. Meyer. Coffee?"

He accepted a cup, then followed her to her office.

"You should know," he said, "I'll only deal with Maddie Cash."

"Hm." Elinor took a sip of her beverage. "Maddie's a wonderful person. How do you know her?"

"She advised me on the preliminaries. She's already done a great deal of work on my behalf. But before we could proceed further, you fired her."

"I did not fire her." Elinor turned her attention to her computer. "I was employing tough love. Let me see what I can do."

"As long as that something involves her being reinstated."

Elinor looked up and bit her lip, as if choosing her words carefully. "Mr. Meyer," she began. Then she frowned and tipped her head. "You care about her."

He felt his face grow warm in the small room. "She could have met your deadline, at my expense. But she chose not to. I won't let you punish her for that."

MADDIE PARKED ON the street in front of Styles Realty, instead of her old assigned spot. She didn't work there anymore, after all. Elinor's voice on the phone had given Maddie no clues as to the reason for the summons. She hoped she hadn't forgotten some important detail before she left.

When she walked in, she was shocked to see Brad and Emily standing in the waiting room.

"Here she is," Brad said, waving towards Elinor's office.

"Maddie." Emily reached for her. "Finally. I've peed three times, waiting for you. We've made a decision. We want the house. The one you found for us. I adore it and I'm not waiting another minute."

Maddie eyed the woman's belly. "Time is of the essence, I imagine. But what about that garage?"

Brad glanced sideways at his wife, then took her hand. "We can always add one later. I was being selfish. Emily loves this house so that's the one we're buying."

Emily clapped her hands. Her excitement was like a knife to Maddie's heart. How she wanted to celebrate this moment with them.

"I'm happy for you, but—" she began.

"I know, I know, you're on leave or something. I don't care. I don't want to deal with Elinor. I want to deal with you. No offense," Emily said hastily, as Elinor approached.

"None taken." She held up a slim folder. "Turns out waiting was the right choice. The seller's dropped the asking price."

Elinor handed the folder to Maddie, a knowing smile tickling her lips.

"Good work, Maddie," she said.

"I don't understand." She felt like there wasn't enough air in the room. What was happening? Did she have her job back?

"You've done the work. Now close the deal. We'll talk later, okay?"

Maddie's throat tightened. "Yeah," she whispered. "Okay."

Elinor leaned her head down as she passed. "First Mr. Meyer, then these two," she murmured. "Welcome back, Maddie. Seems none of us can do without you."

Maddie's head snapped up. Mick? What did he have to do with anything?

IT WAS DARK by the time Maddie sent Brad and Emily home. They had no subjects on their offer and she wasn't expecting a counter. They wouldn't be moved in before the baby arrived, but at least they could stop looking.

The night was clear and cold, with a waxing crescent moon that made the world feel shrouded in black velvet. Her headlights illuminated the road sufficiently, but as she passed Edge's sign, she still felt she was entering uncharted territory.

She hadn't heard from Mick since the night at her apartment and had no idea what she was going to say to him.

It had been over a week since she'd seen the lodge and when she turned onto the long driveway, she saw that someone, Chad probably, had cleared the entire yard. No chance she'd get stranded this time. Smoke rose from the chimney and soft yellow light shone from the new front windows. Logan and his crew had been busy.

Mick was on the porch before she was out of her car. She stood in the dark for a moment, looking at his strong silhouette backlit by the interior light.

"You went to Elinor," she said eventually. Her voice tinkled crisply on the packed snow.

"Come inside, Maddie." He reached out a hand.

"No one's ever stood up for me like that."

"Then it was overdue. Come on. You're going to freeze."

She took a few steps, her feet numb, her heart thumping wildly.

"It's not your place to rescue me, Mick."

"It wasn't your place to rescue me, either. Guess we're even. You hungry? I've got stew from a can. It's not great but it beats a mustard and potato chip sandwich by a landslide. Also, I'm in love with you."

She stumbled and barely caught herself on the porch railing.

"What?"

He was at her side in a flash, and then she was in his arms.

"Homemade stew is better but I didn't have the ingredients."

His lips were on her cheeks, his breath warming her skin. *Love?*

"You smell like chocolate," she said. Her teeth chattered.

"My secret weapon." He tugged her through the doorway. "It's nice to be the sturdy one, for a change."

She surveyed the freshly-painted room, hugging her arms and shivering. "It looks amazing in here. You've been busy.

How are you feeling?"

"Impatient. Let's get you warmed up."

She noticed there were candles on the table, tall ones. And a single rose, in a vase. Two place settings.

"Mick?" She lifted her gaze to his. "What's going on?"

She knew from Cynthia that he was here, but she hadn't told him she was coming.

"You've got more friends than you realize." He lifted the jacket from her shoulders, then walked her to the table and pulled out a chair. "Elinor called Cynthia, who called Sage, who put together this little incentive package and sent it out with Chad. They all seemed to think I had a chance but until I saw your headlights on the yard, I didn't believe it. Sit."

He wasn't the bloodied, raving mess he'd been when they'd met, but there was a hint of the same vulnerability that had stolen her heart that night.

"I left Clementine at the ranch," she said, the words tumbling out. "Just in case. I don't know why. My mom loves her." She paused. "You're in love with me?"

He set a dome-covered plate onto the table. "I lied. Oh, not about that. About the stew." He lifted the lid. "I thought we'd have chocolate, instead."

Dark chocolate covered Himalayan salted caramels. Her favorite.

He lifted a piece and took a bite. A tiny piece of chocolate broke away and fell against his chin. She reached out to catch it.

"Mm," he said, holding out the other half. He licked his lips, slowly, keeping his eyes on her and she felt her resolve crumble.

It wasn't the chocolate that made her mouth water. She knew exactly how it would feel melting on her tongue. Coarse pink granules dotted the dark surface, a surprising salty crunch, and then the sticky slide of smooth, dense chocolate and the silky, chewy caramel inside.

It was Mick. She'd resisted him for so long, closed herself off when everything inside her was screaming that he might actually be the one.

Here he was standing in front of her with his heart on offer.

And chocolate in his hands.

"Of course I love you." Mick held out the remainder, the marks of his teeth visible against the chocolate shell, the golden center oozing slightly. "Open up."

She pulled back. "You're not suddenly going to stay in one spot, become a landowner, and start raising chickens, Mick. If you're trying to change your life, become someone different, for me…" Her throat closed. "Friends accept each other as they are. No conditions."

His dark eyes grew fierce. He took a deep breath, exhaled heavily. "Maddie. You can be so obtuse sometimes. I'm not your friend. I'm in love with you. As in, want to get you naked and paint you with chocolate and then lick it off. I want to go skinny-dipping in the lake with you when spring comes and show you the northern lights in Alaska and wake up every morning with you and nip that bottom lip of yours and make you moan and come apart in my hands."

She couldn't breathe. She couldn't tear her eyes from him. Her pulse beat low and hot in her belly.

"I think you're in love with me too, but I've got five months to convince you, if you're not sure," he continued. "I'm sticking around to see where this goes, Maddie. Maybe I'll set up an outfit on Edge's land, maybe run it with my mom, but I don't know. Once I'm cleared to fly again, I can take a few contract jobs now and then, bring you along, if you're interested. Or, hell, raise chickens. Why not? Wherever you are, that'll be home for me."

He continued talking and she heard words, random bits of data popping up like driftwood in a rushing stream. Hunting cabin. Fire detection. Aerial mapping.

"You... you're really... in love with me?"

"You want me to say it again?"

She couldn't move. Couldn't speak. This wasn't real.

"I was broken," he said, "and you cured me, with lilacs and sunshine and chocolate."

Her chest was shuddering, the little bird trapped inside beating wildly against her ribs.

"You're a miracle, Maddie. You're the best person I've ever known. How could I not love you?" He slipped to his knees in front of her, reaching his hand around the back of her neck and pulling her close.

A sound came from her throat, an awful, involuntary,

clutching cry and then his lips were on hers and she tasted the sweetness of caramel and acceptance and the fulfillment of a heart's desire she'd barely acknowledged.

He cupped the back of her head, then his hands were on her shoulders, in her hair, on her face as if he couldn't get enough of her, wanted to devour her and she gave herself over to the sheer pleasure of his touch. She felt the same.

Finally, they pulled apart, Mick breathing as hard as she was.

"So?" His voice was hoarse. "What do you say? Will you give up those crazy resolutions of yours and just be yourself with me? What were they again?"

Her pulse was pounding in her ears but she felt light, so light that she might float away. "No more chocolate."

He picked up another piece and held it to her lips. "Life's too short to say no to pleasure."

Maddie opened her mouth and he placed it against her tongue. She bit down. The deep, rich flavor, the creamy texture, the sheer sensual bliss washed over her and she moaned. "Okay," she mumbled. "I give up. Wha' about meddling?"

"I love your meddling. Do your worst."

"No more men?"

"Ah," he said, coming in for another kiss. "You can keep that one. Except for me, of course."

"I can do that," she said.

The End

You'll love the rest of…

Love at the Chocolate Shop series

Book 1: *Melt My Heart, Cowboy* by C.J. Carmichael

Book 2: *A Thankful Heart* by Melissa McClone

Book 3: *Montana Secret Santa* by Debra Salonen

Book 4: *The Chocolate Cure* by Roxanne Snopek

Book 5: *The Valentine Quest* by Melissa McClone

Available now at your favorite online retailer!
Find out about the rest of the series here

About the Author

USA TODAY bestselling author Roxanne Snopek writes contemporary romance both sexy and sweet, in small towns, big cities and secluded islands, with families and communities that will warm your heart. Her fictional heroes (like her own real-life hero) are swoon-worthy, uber-responsible, secretly vulnerable and occasionally dough-headed, but animals love them, which makes everything okay. Roxanne writes from British Columbia, Canada, where she is surrounded by wild flowers, wildlife and animals that require regular feeding. She does yoga to stay sane. It works, mostly.

Visit her website at RoxanneSnopke.ca

Thank you for reading

The Chocolate Cure

If you enjoyed this book, you can find more from all our great authors at TulePublishing.com, or from your favorite online retailer.

TULE
PUBLISHING

65896964R00157

Made in the USA
Charleston, SC
07 January 2017